BEHIND THE MASK

EMIKAT JUN

BEHIND THE MASK

EMIKAT JUN

Published by
Wrate's Publishing

BEHIND THE MASK
EMIKAT JUN © 2018

First Published by Wrate's Publishing
ISBN 978-1-9996089-2-7

Edited and typeset by Wrate's Editing Services, London
www.wrateseditingservices.co.uk

Disclaimer
All the characters and many of the events in this book are fictitious.
Any similarity to real persons, living or dead, is coincidental and not
intended by the author.

Dedication
For my dearest parents – Amante E. Ulep, Sr., now resting
peacefully in heaven, and Elizabeth B. Ulep. Thank you for
showing me the true meaning of unconditional love,
and for being my forever mentors in life.

Part One

Chapter One

Maya Wara-Smith sat quite still as she stared at the phone, her large brown eyes wandering blankly between the photoframes behind it. One was of her and Keith on their wedding day, the other was of her seated on top of a big rock, admiring a beautiful waterfall. Jani, one of her Shih Tzu dogs, leapt onto her lap. As she stroked her, horrible scenes came streaming through her mind. Then questions started to pile up one after another. It took her a few minutes to compose herself, then she gently moved Jani to her side and reached for her laptop on the table.

She started to search on the internet for flights. Bingo! There was one leaving Glasgow for Manila at 8pm that evening. She checked the time; it was 2pm and it would take two hours to get to Glasgow from her house. She booked the flight and quickly packed her suitcase. Her husband

Keith, a keen angler, was out fishing with his friends and would not be back until 5pm. No point in phoning him now, his mobile phone would be switched off while he was by the water. Instead, she reached for a pen and paper and scribbled a note for him.

As Maya drove past the beautiful, early spring scenery, she couldn't help but thank the Divine Providence for the lovely, dry day. A week ago, the Highlands were covered with snow and it would have been impossible to drive to Glasgow from Alban within two hours. Maya hoped she'd seen the last of the unforeseen late winter snowfalls.

Halfway through the journey, she stopped to stretch her legs and admire the landscape, which she'd fallen in love with the moment she stepped onto Scottish soil over two decades ago. Springtime had just arrived and the surroundings came alive once again, with countless waterfalls cascading through the rolling hills. The hills were covered with purple-coloured wild lavenders, and made a wonderful sight against a magnificent backdrop of snow-capped mountains. She felt refreshed and carried on with her drive.

Whilst on the road, Maya sighed as she recalled the hurried conversation she'd had earlier with her cousin, Cora Bautista. It was so abrupt that Maya hadn't had a chance to ask any questions. All she'd managed to ascertain was that Cora's five-year-old daughter Nina – her goddaughter – had been abducted by a gang of masked motorcyclists and was feared dead. It was almost incomprehensible, and Maya knew she needed to get to the Philippines as soon as she could.

'My poor, poor cousin. As if she hasn't suffered enough,' she murmured.

Cora's husband Paulo had been a soldier. He was killed during an ambush by the LPG (Likas Punas Group), the country's long-standing communist rebels, while assigned to a mountainous region called the Cordilleras. Cora was pregnant with her second child when he died.

Maya shook her head as she thought about her dearest cousin. How could life be so cruel? Cora had coped very well since losing her husband. Of course, she had struggled to arrange his funeral while heavily pregnant, but the arrival of Nina, a sister to her three-year-old son, Dino, brought new hope and joy. It was clear that Cora's children were her inspiration and the reason for her life.

Cora studied dentistry and started practising soon after she graduated and got her qualifications. She met Paulo, a sergeant of the Philippine army, during a short stint doing work experience in one of the Cordilleras provinces. They were both smitten with each other and married a year later, deciding to settle in Manila, where Cora set up her own private dental clinic near their house while Paulo continued his assignments in different provinces around the country. He came home as often as his bosses would allow, and sometimes they arranged for Cora to stay at his army detachment instead. This was their life for three blissful years until the shocking moment when Cora received the call from Paulo's infantry commander to tell her that he had died during an encounter with the rebels.

Although there were ten years between them, Maya and

Cora were more like sisters or best friends than cousins. Maya's parents had died in a car accident when Maya was ten. Her father, Nicolas Wara, was a lawyer who had become a prominent politician in their town, and her mother, Elizabeth, was a schoolteacher. Their deaths were surrounded by doubt and suspicion. Some said the crash was a result of foul play perpetrated by political rivals during the local election campaign period.

After her parents' deaths, Maya went to live with the family of her mother's only sister, Lina. Auntie Lina and Uncle Larry treated her like their own child. Her cousin Cora was a baby at the time and Maya lived with them happily until she was 18 and went to university in Manila.

It was five o'clock when Maya arrived at Glasgow airport, just in time to check-in for the flight. While waiting to board the plane, she decided to go for a drink at the airport's Wuther's Pub. She was just about to call Keith when her mobile phone rang.

'Hello, honey. Where are you now?' asked her puffed-sounding husband.

'Hon, I'm in the airport pub waiting to board in an hour or so. Did you read …?' Maya started to explain, but Keith interrupted her.

'I'm outside the airport now. Yes, I got your message. I got home earlier than usual because Danny, the novice, felt unwell, so we finished our jigging lessons early. I thought

I'd try and catch you up to see you off.'

'Oh, honey, thank you! Come on over.'

Maya was delighted that she would get to see her husband before she left.

It wasn't long until Maya and Keith had to say their goodbyes. They both agreed that Keith would stay at a friend's house in Glasgow and drive back to the Highlands in the morning. Maya would keep him up-to-date regarding her travels.

It was an eighteen-hour journey to Manila, including a five-hour stopover in Seoul. After dinner on the plane, Maya tried to sleep. She was tired but her mind was active. Every time she went to her homeland, she experienced mixed feelings of excitement and sorrow. This time, it was more complex and worrisome. As always, whenever she had these strong feelings, she let her mind run wild, and slowly memories of bygone years started flooding in.

Chapter Two

Maya was 22 when, in March 1990, she graduated from Luzviminda University in Manila as a summa cum laude (with the highest distinction) in BS Journalism. She was immediately recruited by a leading newspaper company, *The Pinoy News*. Within five years she had worked her way up to Regional Director for the Travel and Tourism department.

During her first year of employment, she met Arthur Manabo, a photographer for the company. They were paired together to cover the news in various remote areas outside Manila, consequently falling madly in love.

But, after seven years of living together, Maya found out that Arthur was seeing another woman, who was expecting his child. This news was a double blow for Maya. Being an only child, she'd always wanted to have a large family, but after trying to conceive for three years without success, they'd both decided to have a medical check-up.

It turned out that Maya was infertile. She clearly remembered the day when they went to get the results and the moment when the doctor, who was very calm and sympathetic, asked them to sit down. Maya's world stopped when he broke the news. She barely heard him when he said, 'There's always adoption or you could try IVF or surrogacy.'

Whatever the doctor was saying wouldn't sink in. She could only just recall holding onto Arthur as he guided her out of the clinic. She didn't go to work for the rest of the week and eventually had to ask for two months' sick leave. Arthur kept reassuring her that everything would be all right. He was adamant that he didn't mind being childless and would always be with her. What a farce!

On the morning she uncovered Arthur's lies, Maya's alarm didn't go off so she overslept and had to rush to get to work. She was almost settled into her day when she realised she had forgotten the folder containing the presentation she was due to give that afternoon for her department's weekly briefing. It was a 45-minute drive back home, but Maya couldn't give her talk without the folder. Arthur had come home very late the previous night and she didn't want to disturb his sleep by asking him to bring the folder to her workplace. After all, he badly needed a rest as he'd been working out of town for most of the previous few weeks.

As she opened the front door of their apartment, she could hear someone talking.

'Babes, yes, I'll be there tonight. I promise ... yes, I will tell her. Don't worry ... I will ... don't cry, babes, don't cry ...'

Maya thought at first she was listening to something on the TV, but then she realised it was Arthur's voice. As she walked into the living room, her long-term partner dropped the phone on the floor. Maya sat on the sofa. The silence in the room was unbearable and it was Maya who broke it with a trembling voice. 'So, what are you going to tell me, Arthur?'

'Hon ...'

'Cut the crap and tell me.'

Arthur sat opposite her. 'Hon, I've got something to tell you ... I ... I have been seeing Rita for the last six months ... and ... she is three months pregnant.'

Rita was a receptionist in the building next to their office. Arthur had introduced her to Maya a few months earlier as a friend. It dawned on her why Rita was always present whenever she and Arthur went out in a group.

'How dare you, you son of a bitch! How dare you!' she said, her eyes fixed in an angry glare.

'I'm really sorry, honey ...' Arthur said, reaching out to try and hold Maya.

'No, don't even touch me!' Maya screamed. 'I want you out of this house today and I don't want to see you ever again!'

Maya grabbed the folder from the dining table and stormed out.

Arthur did what he'd been asked and removed all his

belongings from their shared apartment. After that she did not see or hear from him again. It helped that by then he worked for a different department of the publishing company, which meant there was little chance of them bumping into each other. To Maya's immense relief, she'd never married Arthur, which would have made the whole separation a lot more complicated and costly.

Twelve months on, Maya asked her employers to transfer her to another branch outside Manila. To her delight, the Chief Editor, Eduardo Franco, who was better known as *Tito Eddy*, gave her a special one-year assignment to monitor and write about foreign visitors to the island of Puerto Galla, in the province of Ore Mindalo. Tito Eddy had heard a rumour that the island had a dark side. He was confident that Maya was the best person to uncover whether or not this was true. She was provided with a three-bedroom, well-equipped cottage on the understanding that some colleagues may come to stay every now and then.

'I'm sure you'll like it there, Maya,' Tito Eddy said during their meeting to discuss the assignment. 'Always keep your eyes and ears open and remember that the locals are usually the best source of information for everything.'

As they concluded the meeting, Tito Eddy had an afterthought. 'Of course, if after a couple of months you decide that it's not for you, just let me know.'

Maya gladly agreed. 'I will,' she said. 'But this could be just what I really need. I want to get away from everything that reminds me of that bastard … all the places we went, the life we shared. Hopefully the island will give me a chance to put the past behind me and begin to heal, if that's even possible.'

Chapter Three

Maya arranged to put her apartment up for rent while she was away. She packed three suitcases and left her other personal belongings and her car with her friend Brenda in Manila. It was a two-hour bus journey from the capital to the pier and another hour-and-a-half boat ride to the island. She was joined on the passenger boat by about 30 other people, most of whom were foreign tourists, including Americans, Australians and Europeans. There were a couple of Chinese people too.

'What a lovely place this island is, eh?' one of the male tourists, who was seated next to Maya, commented.

'Yes, it definitely looks beautiful and peaceful from here,' Maya replied. 'This is my first time to the island. How about you and where are you from?'

'Oh, I'm from Australia. I'm a diver and writer. I travel

the world regularly and write about my experiences. This island has one of my few favourite diving spots in the world, and this is my third visit so far.'

A French couple seated nearby joined in the conversation.

'We're also here for the diving experience,' the woman said. 'Our friends were here last year and they absolutely loved it.'

'Wow, that's good to know. I feel a bit left out now,' said Maya. 'If only I was good at being in deep water, I would take diving lessons too. But I'm such a wimp!'

Everyone laughed and the three tourists continued to share their diving experiences as Maya listened with great interest.

The view of the island from the sea was lush and inviting. There was no infrastructure in sight, as the greenery that abounded the island covered it. It was only when the boat approached the dock that the action on the island began to unfold.

As they arrived, Maya bade goodbye to the other passengers and wished them a great holiday. She then collected her luggage and was grateful for the two porters who, for a small fee, helped her carry them up to her cottage.

Maya was pleased to finally be in her new place and start her new life. The cottage was just perfect for her. Built in the traditional Filipino way, big wooden stilts – one on each corner and the fifth in the middle – raised it a metre off the ground and afforded it good views overlooking the town and across to the sea. The walls, floors and ceilings were all made of wood and corrugated iron had been used for the burgundy coloured roof. The external walls were painted green and there was a five-step climb up a wooden stairway to reach the massive veranda, and the front door. A huge hammock had been hung on the veranda, making a perfect spot for relaxing and enjoying the sea views.

The cottage had three bedrooms, a toilet and shower room, a large fitted kitchen-diner and a good-sized living room with a small television in the corner, which meant, to Maya's relief, that the island had electricity provisions. Maya didn't think she could ask for more. The cottage had everything she needed.

Tourists regularly came and went from the other cottages in Maya's compound, but she learned that some stayed for as long as a year or so. She slowly became part of the local community and within a month had befriended some of her neighbours.

One day, Maya felt she needed to cool down, as the temperature had been exceptionally high. She remembered Aida, the lady who ran the little corner shop across from her cottage, telling her that there was a privately owned swimming resort a couple of blocks down the road, which was open to the public for a minimum charge.

After working on her news article, she had her lunch and headed for the resort. It had been a while since she'd been swimming and it felt so good to relax in the water again.

She wasn't a good swimmer, though, and got scared when the water was deeper than her height of five feet.

A young couple were playing with their toddler in the pool when Maya arrived, but they packed up for lunch shortly after she got into the water. She had the pool to herself for a while until a bulky, middle-aged Caucasian man walked into the resort, with a girl of around 10 tagging along. Maya thought how cute it was that a father was taking his daughter for a swim. The man sat by the restaurant near the pool, kissed his daughter on the lips and ushered her to the pool as Maya swam back and forth across the shallow end, soaking up the heat of the sun that was tempered by the coolness of the water. 'This is bliss,' she thought.

Maya eventually noticed the girl hovering nearby. She wasn't swimming, but rather gliding along the edges of the pool.

'Hi,' Maya said.

As the girl was about to open her mouth to say something, her father, who was by this time drinking with another man, shouted her name. Maya couldn't make out what it was, as the man's accent was quite strong.

'Yes, Pa,' the girl shouted back and moved away from Maya.

Maya finally had enough of swimming and decided to pack it up. As she showered in the open-ended, women-only shower room, the girl followed suit and turned on the shower next to her. Maya felt a bit uneasy, as she seemed to be watching her. Finally, she spoke.

'What's your name, *Ate*?'

'Maya, what's yours?'

'My name is Edith and I'm nine years old. How old are you, *Ate*?'

'Oh, I'm much older than you. Why?'

'I'm just asking. You have big boobs, *Ate*. I like your swimsuit and your long black hair.'

Maya was taken aback. Why would a nine year old talk about feminine parts to a stranger? It was odd.

'Oh, thank you, you are a lovely girl and you'll have big boobs too when you grow older,' Maya said, which made the girl smile. 'Mind you,' she added, 'you'll grow a lot taller too – just like your father.'

'My father is dead,' the girl said, her face dropping.

'Oh, I am sorry, dear. Who is the man you came here with, then? I heard you called him Pa.'

'Oh, that's Papa Herman, *Ate*. He's my mama's boyfriend. He's from Germany.'

Then Edith leant towards Maya and, almost whispering, added, 'You want to know something? He's got a very big dick!'

Maya was totally shocked by what she'd just heard. As she struggled to find words to say, she heard shouting outside the shower room. It was Papa Herman calling Edith's name and uttering some words in broken English.

'I'm coming, Papa,' Edith called back, before rushing out of the shower block.

As she walked back to her cottage, Maya couldn't stop thinking about her disconcerting encounter with young

Edith. Could what she'd heard be true? Were men flocking to the island for more than just the diving?

'Please, God, let it not be true,' Maya whispered quietly to herself.

Chapter Four

By the time she was approaching her second month on the island, Maya had settled right in. One sunny afternoon, she decided to tackle the one-hour hike up Cava Hill, to see the bat cave people had been talking about.

As she approached the mouth of the cave, she heard some grunting noises in what she thought was a foreign tongue. Whoever the voice belonged to was obviously in pain.

'Urgh ... oh, shit ... this ... oh, fuck!'

Maya raced to the cave. As she looked inside, she saw a flicker of light in the far end corner.

'Hello?' she called out.

As soon as she spoke, a batch of bats took flight, creating a deafening, squeaky sound that echoed around the space. Maya stooped down and almost hit her head on a rock in front of her. As she pressed on, she tried to avoid the tiny mammals flying towards her face.

The light inside the cave diminished once she had passed through the entrance, and she could barely see ahead of her. She reached out for her pocket torch, calling out at the same time.

She heard some human noises in response and pointed her torch in the direction they were coming from. She saw two figures in the corner where she'd spotted the flicker of light earlier.

'Thank goodness someone is out there!' a man shouted. He was speaking in English, with an accent Maya couldn't place. 'We're in here and I need a bit of help. I fell off that rock over there and I think I've sprained my ankle. Be careful yourself, it is very slippery.'

'I'm on my way!' Maya shouted back, as she slowly walked towards the big rock where the voice was coming from. Behind it was a slope towards the little chamber where the two figures were seated. One was a lot smaller and, as he looked up towards Maya, she could make out that he was a teenage boy. His arms were stretched around the man's body, as he tried desperately to lift him up.

'Hold on a minute, I'll be back,' Maya shouted. She fumbled through her knapsack for her emergency medical kit and the rope she always carried with her. As a journalist, one of her mantras was to always be prepared. It helped that she'd also been a girl scout. She retreated from the cave and looked for a tree branch that was big and sturdy enough for the man to use as a cane. When she found one, she used the rope to hook it and bring it down.

Back inside the cave, she could hear the man cursing and swearing with frustration and pain. She studied the areas around the cave with her torch and came to the conclusion that everywhere was quite rocky. However, she saw that there was an easier way to avoid the slippery slope and slowly climbed down the hollow.

The injured man could hardly move his left foot, but he seemed to have calmed down. He was wearing shorts and walking sandals and his thighs and knees were badly scratched and bruised. Maya removed the sandal from his left foot, in preparation to treat the injury, and took out a bandage from her medical kit. The boy quietly assisted her as she began to wrap it around the man's ankle. They were silent for a few minutes as they got on with what they had to do.

'Are you a doctor?' the man asked.

'No,' replied Maya.

'A nurse?'

'No, I'm a journalist and I happen to know a bit of first aid, so don't worry. I know what I'm doing, sir.'

'Oh, of course. I'm sorry. I didn't mean to question your ability. My name is Keith Smith by the way. I'm a photographer. And I am stupid, I know. I should have known better and prepared myself to come here. It's very unlike me to get into this state. Anyway, thank you for helping. You are a godsend, I owe you big time.'

'No worries. My name is Maya. Hold on a minute …' She climbed up a stretch of rock thin enough to wrap one end of the rope around. Then she climbed back down and handed the other end to Keith. ' … Now, hold on to this as we pull you up to stand, OK?'

It took several tries before Keith could get his balance enough to stand up. Maya gave him her makeshift wooden cane to lean on, as he stood and lifted his bandaged left foot off the ground. Maya and the boy quietly assisted him as he walked painfully and slowly out of the cave.

Once they were outside, the boy started to talk. It was clear that he was close to tears.

'*Ate*, he was taking photos and didn't see there was a gap between the rocks he was standing on. I tried to tell him, but it was too late. It's my fault. My father was supposed to show Mr Smith inside the cave, but he isn't well. I volunteered as we need the money to buy his medicine. My name is Junior, *Ate*.'

Maya felt a pang in her chest as she listened to Junior's account.

'It's OK,' she soothed. 'We cannot carry Mr Smith down the hill and he won't manage it hopping on one leg. He needs to be carried down by two or three people. Can you run down to the town and ask for help?'

Feeling relieved that there was something he could do, Junior agreed and, after a quick glance at Mr Smith, who in turn nodded, he rushed off.

As Keith Smith leant over a rock, the pain he felt

was painted on his face. He also felt totally stupid and embarrassed. After all the years of training in difficult terrains and in far more challenging places, this was the worst pain he'd ever felt in his ankle. He thought he might have broken a bone or torn a ligament. However, he could move his toes a little, so he hoped it was just shock and a very bad sprain.

As if reading his mind, Maya offered him some painkillers.

'I have some paracetamol if you want. They may help.'

'Yes please, thank you,' Keith replied, forcing a smile. Maya handed him two tablets to take with her water. He gulped them down and nearly emptied the water bottle.

'How long had you been inside the cave?'

'We left my hotel at nine this morning and got here about ten.'

'Oh dear, that's over five hours ago now,' said Maya. Keith nodded.

Maya couldn't wait for help to come. She felt a bit awkward about being alone with this total stranger. She avoided looking at him directly and a silence ensued between them. Keith tried hard to control his pain and couldn't help but admire the girl beside him.

'I'm sorry, Miss Maya,' he said. 'I've ruined your plans for the day.'

'No worries, it's been part of my daily adventure I guess. Nowadays, I'm kind of used to strange surprises.'

'I remember you saying earlier that you're a journalist. Are you here on the island to cover a particular topic?'

'Sort of,' Maya replied. 'I write about travel and tourism.'

'Wow! I could be one of your cases then, ha ha – "A stupid foreigner photographer slipped into the cave ... "'

Maya laughed. 'Mmmm, not a bad idea. I think I will!'

Just then, four men arrived with a DIY stretcher made up of a piece of canvas and two pieces of pole-shaped hardwood. Keith Smith wasn't a small man. At six feet tall, he weighed around sixteen stone. Maya was grateful there were four men to help. Keith felt helpless, but he knew there was no way he could manage hopping down the rugged and narrow terrain. He would have to trust his life to these strangers. Maya spoke to the men and one of them introduced himself as Carlos. He was one of the island's *barangay* officers. He and the others meticulously prepared the stretcher and Keith lay on it so the men could carry him away.

Maya wanted to stay for a little while and have a good look inside the cave. She bid Keith farewell and told him to get well soon.

'Thanks again,' Keith said. 'I hope to see you again soon.'

It wasn't long before Maya exited the cave once more. She'd had enough of the bats already and didn't have the heart to go deeper into the cave. She may not have liked them flapping around her face, but she thought it was wonderful that bats had a home on the island. She'd heard of other places where the mammals were a delicacy and hunted regularly, hence their decline in population.

As Maya carefully trekked back to the island's town, she spotted a little path along the dirt track. Intrigued, and as it was still daylight, she followed it. About 300-metres on she heard a faint trickle of water, which became louder as she continued her walk. The little path led her to a huge rock, which she had to climb over. When she reached the other side, she found herself in awe of what was in front of her.

About 100-metres away was a magnificent waterfall. Maya found a spot to sit down as she tried to soak in the beauty of the scenery. The waterfall was over 500-metres high and was nestled in the middle of lush greenery, as if dividing the east and west of the island's forest.

Maya reflected how some of the trees on either side could easily be over 100 years old. They were tall, bulky, leafy and very dominating. Maya pondered how there seemed to be an air of mystery about them. The drop of the waterfall formed a whirlpool surrounded by a clear, mini pool, before the waters continued to cascade downstream. Maya was tempted to take a dip … if only she had more time. By then it was nearly six and she thought she better head back to the cottage before sunset.

The next day, Maya checked some local magazines and brochures to see if there was anything about the waterfall she'd come across. She didn't find anything and thought about writing an article about it herself. She started jotting down some notes, wondering why it hadn't been promoted or even mentioned in any of the brochures she'd leafed through.

She had to buy some bread and went along to her neighbouring shop.

'Do you know about the waterfall near the cave?' she asked Aida.

'Ah, you found that place!' Aida hesitated at first, before adding, 'Listen, nobody speaks much about it. Legend says a mermaid called Lavinia lived there for centuries and, in order to stay alive, she had to periodically sacrifice someone. Three people have died going into that pool in the last two years alone. I went once when I was a teenager, but I didn't stay long – it was too scary.'

Aida was clearly distressed by the subject, but she continued anyway. 'It's a shame because it's a very beautiful spot to visit, but the islanders are very superstitious, hence people tend to avoid it. They don't even recommend it for tourists. You were very brave going there on your own.'

Maya was not the superstitious type, but she still shivered when she realised what could have happened if she'd gone into the pool. When she got back to the cottage, she crossed out the article she had just started to write…

Chapter Five

A couple of weeks after the cave incident, Maya was walking towards the beach when someone called for her attention.

'*Ate* Maya, wait!' It was Junior. '*Ate*, I have been trying to find you. Mr Smith told me to give you this note. He went to a hospital in Manila for treatment the day after the accident. He wanted to see you before he left but he did not know where you lived.'

'Oh, thank you, Junior. How are you and how is your father?'

'I'm fine, *Ate*, and Papa is a lot better now. He went back to work on his boat on Monday. That's what he mainly does for a living and I go with him at the weekends. Yesterday, we had a good catch and the Beachfront Hotel bought it all.' Junior said all this with a big grin on his face.

Maya thought how different Junior was from the timid teen she'd met in the cave.

'Oh, that's wonderful. But I thought your father was a tour guide?'

'He does that every now and then. Some tourists want to hire his boat to go fishing. Mr Smith was his last customer and he asked Papa if he could take him to the cave one day … well, you know what happened then … ' Junior looked down.

'Oh, I see. But don't feel bad about it. What happened in the cave wasn't your fault.'

This brought Junior back to being his talkative self again. 'Yes, *Ate*, Mr Smith kept saying that to me too. You know he insisted on paying me his fee. I hesitated to accept it at first, but then it did help to buy my Papa's medicine. He's much better now. I just hope Mr Smith gets well soon too. We've not heard from him since he and another white man left for Manila.'

Junior looked back to where he'd just come from.

'*Ate*, I'm sorry, but I need to go. Papa and I are going fishing again soon.'

'OK, Junior, thank you very much for this note and for talking to me.'

Maya was grateful to have seen Junior, as he'd really brightened up her Sunday morning. She realised what a clever boy he was. 'By the way, I'm staying at number 17 Hilltop Cottages, in case you need to see or talk to me again. Take care now.'

'You're welcome, *Ate*. Thank you too and see you around.'

After Junior had sped off, Maya continued her stroll by the beach and remembered to read the note Keith had left her.

> *Dear Maya, to be on the safe side, I have to get my ankle X-rayed, so I'm going to a hospital in Manila. My friend, Mr Davies, is taking me there. I wanted to see you first before I left, but I totally forgot to ask where you're staying. I'm at the Beachfront Hotel. I would like to treat you to dinner when I come back, just to thank you for saving my life.*
> *Take care,*
> *Keith Smith*

Maya smiled and put the note inside her pocket. For the past two weeks, she'd been busy writing her articles for *The Pinoy News Saturday Special* edition. Every week, as part of her employment agreement, she had to send her work, via the PHL Courier Services, to the Chief Editor, Tito Eddy. She sometimes wished there was an easier way to send them, as they could be bulky and the courier charged extortionate fees. She'd been so preoccupied with all this that she'd all but forgotten about the cave incident and Keith. Her encounter with Junior had jogged her memory.

She carried on walking and after a couple of miles spotted the Beachfront Hotel. She'd strolled along the beach before but hadn't really explored this part of the island. She found it very quiet and peaceful and wondered how busy it became during the day.

The hotel was very attractive and painted yellow, red and blue. It looked huge and Maya thought how the hundreds of people checked in would soon be filling the beautiful beach.

She headed back to her cottage using the island road. She noticed a local bakery, Panaderia, on her way and decided to buy some of their *pandesal* bread for her breakfast.

Chapter Six

Maya's daily routine on the island had only been broken once – when she had an unprecedented encounter with a man in a cave. For this reason, she felt a sense of relief when two colleagues came to stay in the cottage with her: Edward, a photographer, and Gina, a budding young reporter who Maya could immediately tell was full of enthusiasm. Gina reminded Maya of herself when she was starting out in her career years earlier.

The two colleagues had been sent to the island to cover a diving festival. Maya was glad to have some company for a change. After a few months of solitude, it was really good to be with other people and share jokes and experiences.

On their first evening together they relaxed on the veranda and Gina excitedly climbed into the hammock.

'Oh, wow!' she said. 'This is the life! How relaxing to be

able to sit in this gorgeous spot after a hectic day at work. I'd never tire of it here.'

Edward, who was sitting on a chair next to Maya, readily agreed. 'Definitely!' he said. 'It would surely give me the motivation to work every day. By the way, Gina, if you ever get assigned to any other jobs on an island like this one, do make sure I'm your partner photographer, eh?'

'Sure I will. My ever present paparazzo!' Gina joked.

'Watch yourselves, you two. If you're constantly together, Mr Cupid might work his magic,' Maya teased.

'Not in a million, Maya!' Edward protested. 'I am a very happily married man with three lovely kids.'

Gina suddenly sat herself up in the hammock and declared, with a smile on her face: 'For the record, I'd rather be a spinster than go out with this guy – lovely as he is!'

The International Diving Association had been hosting an annual event for various diving clubs around the world since its conception in the early 80s. This was the first time it was being held in the Philippines, with Puerto Galla picked as the fortunate venue.

For seven days, the island was teeming with sports enthusiasts and spectators alike. Maya and her colleagues reckoned all the hotels and accommodation on the island were fully booked. This was good publicity in general and would financially benefit the islanders, as well as the local authority.

Maya, Edward and Gina attended every event. At night, they spent their time debating what details and photographs to feature in their news articles. It was decided that Maya would write a review of the whole event.

By the end of the week, they were all knackered. On the night before Edward and Gina were due to leave the island, they decided to wind down at a disco pub near the Beachfront Hotel. After their dinner, they made their way to the beach and strolled towards the venue, with Maya and Gina barefoot and carrying their heeled sandals.

They took their time and Edward enjoyed the freedom of taking photos for fun rather than for work. Gina was in awe of the island's beauty and was adamant she'd return for a holiday one day. The scenery was as inspiring as ever, with the sunset surrounded by a kaleidoscope of bright red and orange colours; the reflection of them on the wide blue sea was out of this world.

'I would never tire of being here, it's magic!' Gina said again.

The disco pub was just starting to fill up when they arrived at 8pm. The dance floor didn't open for another hour so they bought a bottle of beer each and went outside to sit on some chairs set out under an Acacia tree. Some locals and tourists came to chat with them and the topic of the night was naturally the festival.

When the music started up people gradually wandered

inside. Maya and her colleagues were following suit when she heard a familiar voice calling her name. She spun around and saw a man walking towards them.

'Hello, Maya! It's Keith … Keith Smith, remember?'

'Oh yes, of course, I remember,' Maya replied, feeling a little awkward. She hadn't actually recognised him at all. It had been four months since their first encounter and Keith was now clean-shaven and looked totally different to the man she'd met in the cave. She thought how handsome he looked in his navy blue polo shirt and jeans. Maya had barely thought about him since the day Junior had given her his note.

'May I join you? I'm on my own,' he said, looking towards Maya's companions, who both nodded.

Maya introduced them. 'They came here for the diving festival and are leaving tomorrow,' she explained. 'We thought we'd come here for a little celebration. It's been a hectic week.'

'Cool, nice to meet you both,' Keith smiled, shaking hands with Gina first and then Edward.

'I'm also a photographer,' he said to Edward. 'Not a perfect one, but I try.'

'I think I know what you mean,' Edward laughed and they all went inside.

The four of them managed to squeeze in amongst the hundreds of partygoers. The seats were all taken, but they were able to find a corner near the bar and watch the action from there.

The music was loud and they could hardly hear one

another. Keith ordered drinks for all of them and it wasn't long before Maya and Gina graced the dance floor.

'How did you meet Keith?' Gina asked. 'He is quite handsome, eh? A bit like Bruce Willis in *Die Hard*.'

'I met him inside a cave,' said Maya.

Gina's eyes widened. 'What?'

'Yes, he'd hurt himself and I helped him,' Maya explained.

'Oh, my, that's very romantic!' Gina said, a big grin spreading across her face.

'Stop it, you! I hardly know him. He could be married for all I know. Besides, I'm not ready or interested in anything like that. I like being by myself at the moment.'

'Oh well, Maya, you never know ... '

Gina pressed on, but Maya just shook her head. She was feeling so happy that night; it had been a long time since she'd been out to a disco. She loved dancing and back in Manila she used to go with Arthur and some friends at least once a month. When the memory of Arthur made an appearance she quickly brushed it aside and carried on dancing with Gina, determined that nothing would dampen her high spirits.

Before long, Edward and Keith came to join them. They had fun dancing and singing along to the music as Edward and Keith showed off their wacky moves. Then all of the sudden the music changed and a spotlight was directed to a small stage. Three half-naked ladies walked in as the curtains opened and seductively danced towards three poles.

Maya was horrified. She quickly used her hand to cover

her mouth, which had fallen open.

'They are pole dancers, Maya,' Gina laughed. 'Have you not seen them perform before? This is my third time and it's very interesting. However, the ones I saw before were wearing sexy dresses and weren't half naked!'

Maya looked at Edward and Keith in turn. They were both looking at the stage with a hint of amusement on their faces.

Keith turned around and caught Maya looking at him. 'Are you OK?' he asked.

Maya shook her head. 'I think I'll head back to the cottage now, I'm tired.'

'I'm coming with you,' Gina butted in and Edward said the same.

'I'm getting tired too,' Keith added. 'I only arrived from Manila this afternoon. It's time for a good rest.'

They walked outside together. Keith thanked them for a great night and wished Edward and Gina a safe journey the next day. 'Did you get my note by any chance?' he asked Maya.

'Yes, I did,' Maya replied.

'So, how about that dinner I owe you? When are you available?'

'Well, erm, probably tomorrow night.' Maya said, realising she would be on her own by then and missing her colleagues' company.

'Perfect! You can come over to the Beachfront Hotel at six tomorrow evening, if that suits you? I will book us a table.'

'Yeah, that will be great,' Maya agreed.

They bade each other goodnight and Keith walked towards the hotel. The trio began their 15-minute walk back to the cottage, using the island road this time. As they walked, Gina quizzed Maya for more details about her first meeting with Keith and she duly obliged. Edward smiled as he listened to his two giggly colleagues. By the time they reached the cottage, Maya was exhausted and went straight up to bed.

Chapter Seven

Gina and Edward left the island the following morning, as planned. Maya went to see them off. The cottage was very quiet when she returned and it felt strange to be on her own again. She tried to shrug off her sadness and told herself she would get used to it again soon enough.

Even though it was Saturday she got out her typewriter and started a new article entitled: *An Island's Love Affair with Tourists*. Then she changed it to: *Tourists' Love Affair with an Island*.

She was glad to be up-to-date with all her other work, including the review of the diving festival. She'd sent them all to Tito Eddy via Gina and Edward, which had saved her a few hundred pesos in courier charges.

She did not notice the time until it reached four in the

afternoon. She was meeting up with Keith at six so she packed up her writing stuff and started to get ready. Then she took a *tricycle* to the hotel. She was glad to be using this wonderful three-wheeled vehicle again, which was powered by a motorcycle. During her high school days, when she'd lived in the provinces, the tricycle had been her favourite mode of public transport and it brought back some happy memories.

When she arrived, Keith was already waiting for her at reception. He was wearing a black shirt tucked into belted, dark-coloured jeans. His muscular arms were prominent and he looked more attractive than he had done the previous evening. Maya smiled and had to remind herself to be careful about her feelings – this was strictly a friendly meeting.

'You look stunning,' Keith said when he came over to greet her.

'Thank you,' Maya replied. She couldn't bring herself to tell Keith how handsome she thought he looked.

Maya had chosen a simple dark blue dress and coupled it with a pair of black high heels. She'd let her long, straight, jet-black hair hang loose and had brought with her a little black cardigan in case it got cold later on.

'Let's head this way, I'm starving,' Keith said and led Maya further into the building.

Maya was mesmerized by the hotel's interior. The hall to the reception was very spacious and adorned with decorations influenced by the Victorian era. There was a grand staircase to the left-hand side and a massive Italian chandelier lit the stairwell. Maya reckoned this must be an expensive hotel.

The restaurant was on the first floor and it had huge glass windows with great views. From where they were seated, Maya could see the sun setting. She ordered a mixed seafood dish with rice while Keith opted for a whole lobster with potato and salad. Maya's eyes widened when their meals came and the giant crustacean was served. Her expression made Keith laugh. 'It's OK, it doesn't bite,' he said.

For dessert, they both went for the banana split. They enjoyed their meal and ordered a few drinks afterwards, as the conversation flowed. Keith expressed his gratitude one more time for Maya's impromptu rescue operation. 'It could have turned out a lot worse,' he said.

'Well, anyone would have done the same. I just happened to have been there.'

'Yes, you're my angel,' Keith teased.

'If you say so,' she countered.

Keith explained to Maya how he had severely sprained his ankle in the fall and a couple of his toes were badly injured, too. The doctors had even suggested surgery to amputate the toes and save the others, but Keith insisted on keeping them. He had to wear a plaster cast on his injured leg for six weeks. Fortunately, the toes healed well, but he required a further month of physiotherapy before being given a clean bill of health. After that he remained in Manila to attend to other work-related issues.

The restaurant was emptying and Maya checked her

watch; it was nearly nine. 'This has been a lovely evening, thank you, Keith, but I have to leave soon, the tricycles don't take passengers after ten.'

'I had a lovely time, too. I can walk you back to your place if you like?'

'There's no need. Thank you anyway.'

Keith accompanied Maya outside to get a tricycle. They waited for half an hour but nothing came along, so Maya was forced to accept Keith's offer to walk her home. She walked barefoot and carried her high heels to save her feet. Even though she'd only had two glasses of wine she still felt tipsy. Keith had to hold her as they walked. As they joked and giggled together, they looked like lovers having a fun night out. Maya was grateful there were some streetlights on the road.

As they approached her compound, Maya stopped in her tracks. She could hear someone crying from a cottage across the road. Keith stopped to listen too. They heard a man shouting and cursing in English – he was obviously a foreigner – and the woman kept crying.

'Hmmm, lovers' quarrel, maybe,' Keith said and motioned to Maya to walk on. They continued on their way, but Maya's thoughts were with the woman. She couldn't help feeling there was something more to it … the woman wasn't just crying, she was wailing.

When they reached the cottage, Maya's feet were sore from walking barefoot on the cement road. She felt guilty that Keith had to walk back to the hotel so late at night, so she offered him one of the spare rooms to stay in. She was glad she'd tidied them up and changed the beddings right after her colleagues left. Keith was thankful; he didn't fancy walking back so late.

The wine had hit Maya so much that once she got inside her bedroom she fell asleep right away.

☙

When Maya woke up the next morning, Keith was sitting on the veranda. 'Good morning,' she said.

'Did you sleep well?' Keith asked.

'Very well, thanks,' Maya replied. 'And you?'

'I did, thank you. By the way, this is a very beautiful spot you have here. I could sit here all day enjoying the perfect view.'

'Oh, yes, I love it here,' Maya concurred. 'I'm going to make coffee, do you want a cup?'

'Yes please,' Keith replied.

Keith realised it was Sunday and as he had nothing planned for the day he asked Maya if she wanted to go for a walk somewhere on the island. Maya was also free and had an idea about where they could go. They agreed to meet up after lunchtime.

'Oh, by the way, you may want to wear light walking gear,' Maya reminded Keith as he prepared to go back to the hotel.

Chapter Eight

The hottest time of the day had just passed when Maya and Keith began their walk. Keith had dressed in khaki, three-quarter length shorts, a white vest and a pair of walking shoes. He was carrying a small knapsack for his bottled drinking water and an extra shirt. A harness around his chest held his bulky camera. Maya had opted for a pair of light green trousers and a white t-shirt. She was also wearing walking shoes and carrying a small knapsack containing her usual adventure stuff and drinking water. She had tied her long hair into a bun, which was now hidden under her favourite brown hat.

They were just about to climb up a hill when Keith stopped and said, 'Hey, this looks familiar to me. Are we going to the cave again?'

'No, it's a secret. Just follow me,' Maya smiled.

Keith was intrigued. But most of all he was intrigued by this girl. He liked her a lot, but didn't want to appear too forward.

'So, are you going to stay on this island forever?' he asked, beginning his attempt to get to know her better.

'Well, I've only been here for six months now. I work for *The Pinoy News* and they've sent me here for a one-year special assignment. Correction, I actually asked to be relocated temporarily, for personal and recovery reasons.'

'Oh, I see.'

'And to answer your question, yes, I would love to live here forever, if I had the chance. Who wouldn't? It's such a beautiful place.'

'I agree, it's an enchanting location to live,' Keith smiled. 'I'm also here temporarily, but I have no definite timescale. I've been back and forth here since last year, but I may be sent somewhere else at short notice.'

'Really? Being moved constantly must be hard for you and your family.'

'Yeah, it is hard sometimes, but we've gotten used to it,' Keith replied.

They continued walking. Maya was relieved that Keith had a family. That would make her feelings easier to shield.

On the other hand, Keith was trying to figure out how he would tell Maya about his family situation. He was also wondering if Maya had a family of her own.

The dirt track had improved since the last time they walked on it. It was wider and some of the bushes on both sides had been trimmed. The ground had also been levelled and was easier to walk on. Maya got a little disorientated concerning the location of the small path she'd taken to the waterfall. It seemed they had walked for much longer than she'd anticipated. A couple of miles on, she spotted the tiny path and stopped. 'Listen,' she said to Keith, 'we're going to see a place that's unknown to most tourists unless they stumble across it during their walks … '

Maya went on to explain the myth about the mermaid Lavinia. 'This place is so beautiful that I wanted to show it to you. I didn't have time to bring my colleagues here, unfortunately. I think it is a sacred place and it's definitely not a cursed one.'

Maya motioned Keith towards the small path.

'I am even more excited and intrigued now,' he said.

They reached the top of the rock that Maya had previously visited.

'Oh, wow, this is magnificent!' Keith said.

He stood still for a while in complete astonishment as he tried to soak in the wonders around him. Then he remembered his camera. 'I've got to take photos of this,' he said excitedly.

Maya couldn't help but smile. She was delighted someone else was admiring this beautiful place. She sat in the same spot as before and watched nature at its best. The sound of the cascading waterfall combined with birdsong and the stridulating noise of crickets was both relaxing and mystical. She was deep in happy thoughts and smiling when she noticed Keith taking a picture of her. Then he sat down beside her.

'This is definitely a one in a million spot,' he said, continuing to give his own assessment of the place. 'The pool is so inviting and I can't blame people for wanting to dive in there for a swim. I'm very tempted to go in too, but I won't because of what you said. I'm not fearful of the whirlpool, but I respect nature and the locals' belief. I think that people, especially the tourists, should come here and enjoy the view. But they should be warned of the dangers of the whirlpool and be informed of the locals' folklore. I'm sure they would respect that too.'

'I totally agree,' Maya smiled.

She got out her bottled water and some peanuts and biscuits she'd brought along, offering them to Keith. They sat munching their snacks, both lost in their own thoughts for a while.

Then Keith took this moment to tell Maya about his life. 'I was born in Alban in the Scottish Highlands,' he explained. 'My parents decided to move to Yorkshire, England, when I was 10 and my father started to have health problems and couldn't carry on his farm work. Since I was a boy, I've been interested in photography and arts.' He glanced at Maya, who was eagerly listening, before continuing. 'I went to Queens University and finished with a Bachelor of Arts and Humanities when I was 21. After graduating, instead of getting an office job, I decided to join the Royal Air Force. I thought it would be more exciting, and lo and behold I soon learned that it was, but it was extremely tough, too. Don't get me wrong, I still enjoyed it very much and I wouldn't change it for anything. Some of my colleagues at the time couldn't make it to the end, though. Out of the 20 trainees in my class, only 11 of us completed the full 18-months of gruelling training.

'After ten years in the force, I left and joined the Special Royal Security Unit, where I was given the opportunity to go to South Africa. I loved it there ... the weather, the food, the culture, everything, so I decided to stay.'

At this point, Keith took a deep breath and threw some peanuts into his mouth. He smiled at Maya, who was still listening intently while munching on her snacks.

'Well, I ... I got married to Jennifer, an English born South African. We had a daughter together, Penelope. I call her Penny, as I think it suits her better.' He stopped to take another sip from his water bottle. 'However, my job involved constant travel to different countries and after five years our marriage broke down. We divorced but remained friendly towards each other, as best we could anyway. I love my little Penny and she's the beacon of my life. I go back to South Africa to see her whenever I can.'

Keith's face lit up as he talked about his daughter. Maya sensed that he missed her and this made her smile.

'Just where does the time go?' Keith continued. 'I'm coming up to 40 and I can't believe it. I can't wait to retire and go back to my beloved Alban.'

Keith, feeling relieved, had another sip of water and ate some more snacks.

Maya had loved listening to Keith, but she didn't yet feel ready to tell him her own life story. She reminded herself to hold her guard, especially when he recounted how his marriage had broken down. She sensed she was growing to like him, but she was still cautious. The last thing she wanted was to end up getting hurt again.

'Going back to your birth country when you retire would be very exciting,' she said.

'Oh, yes, indeed,' Keith replied. 'I guess you've grown used to being away from your family, too?' he asked.

'Well, yes, but I prefer to be on my own at the moment.'

She'd been dreading this question and wished her answer had sounded more convincing.

'Oh, I see,' Keith muttered.

Feeling awkward for not telling her own story, Maya checked her watch and said, 'I think it's time to head back to town now. It's nearly four thirty.'

'Oh, yes, of course,' Keith agreed. 'I really enjoyed today. Thank you so much for bringing me here.'

'My pleasure,' Maya replied, trying desperately to avoid his gaze.

On their way back to town, Keith took a detour to walk Maya back to her cottage. 'Thank you again, sweetie,' he said and kissed her on the cheek.

The gesture took Maya by surprise. 'You're welcome,' she managed to say and Keith headed back to his hotel.

That night, Maya couldn't sleep. The events of the day

filled her thoughts. How could she be falling for this man? 'I'm scared to open my heart again,' she thought to herself.

They met again the following Saturday afternoon, when Keith came to the cottage to ask Maya to go for a walk on the beach with him; an offer she gladly accepted. It was drizzly and cloudy, but they had a good time nevertheless. They walked almost the whole length of the island's shore, stopping for ice cream and snacks at the small, beachfront stalls along their way. It had been a long time since Maya had felt so relaxed and happy in the company of a man. Keith mentioned how he had been extremely busy the previous week and under intense pressure from his head office in London. 'I badly needed this time to chill,' he said.

Maya briefly wondered how his photography job could put him under so much pressure, but she decided not to press him. After their walk, they went for a swim in the sea. Keith headed right out while Maya stayed near the shore. They were still soaking wet on the walk to Maya's cottage. After dropping her off, Keith continued on to his hotel.

Chapter Nine

An early morning knock on her cottage door the following Monday morning woke Maya from her slumber. She opened it to find two young and well-built men standing outside. One of them showed Maya his ID and he confirmed they were from the IB (Intelligence Bureau). The other one handed Maya an envelope.

'Mr Smith asked us to give you this note,' he said with a hint of authority in his voice. 'He had to leave for Manila at dawn and didn't want to disturb you too early.'

Maya was still half asleep and could barely comprehend what was going on. 'Thank you, officers,' she said. 'Is he all right, I mean, is Mr Smith OK?'

'Yes he is, ma'am. He asked for you not to worry and to trust him.'

With that the two officers said goodbye and briskly walked away.

The note was very short.

Maya, sweetie, I need to go to Manila urgently. Hope to be back soon. Keith xx

For the next two weeks, Maya felt very anxious and could hardly concentrate on her work. She started an article about the myth of the waterfall and its resident mermaid, but was still unsure whether it was appropriate to write about it. She was concerned the locals might react negatively when their secret was exposed.

She put the article off and instead concentrated on her usual topics about the influx of foreigners coming to the island. In normal circumstances, she went to the docking port every other day to collect information on the number of tourists coming and going, the reasons for their journey and their expectations about the island. Sometimes she talked to the new arrivals and shared tips about the island. Many of the people she spoke to were enthusiastic and excited. However, a few would just shrug her questions off, as if it was none of her business.

She collated the information she gathered each week and wrote a summary of it for her articles, which she sent to her editor at the Manila head office. That was her regular routine, but the last two weeks had been different. She'd started going to the docking port every day to get her information, always with the hope of encountering Keith in the process.

In the last few years, *The Pinoy News* (PN) had expanded. It had a broadcasting department (television and radio), where her colleagues Edward and Gina worked. In addition to the daily tabloid they usually brought out, the editorial output had expanded to offer a Saturday edition, which Maya's articles appeared in.

She usually had her copy delivered to her cottage, but one Saturday morning she went to the shop to get some bread and was able to scan through the pages of some other newspapers in the shop. An article in the *SunStar* paper caught her eye. In the corner of page three was a very brief article:

A paedophile ring called Karnal is being investigated in the Far East. Apparently, their centre is in Puerto Galla. How true is this?

Maya was more than a little shaken by what she'd read. She scanned the whole paper to see if there was any more information about it, but couldn't find anything. For the rest of the day she remained pensive. There were so many questions flowing through her mind. How could she have been so naïve and not have investigated this more? She briefly thought of Edith … and then, wait a minute, she'd not seen or heard of Keith since the IB agents had visited her cottage.

'Oh my, oh dear,' she mumbled. 'Oh no, not him, he couldn't be one of them!'

Maya started to draw an outline. She had a plan.

PART TWO

Chapter Ten

A few days later, Maya decided to stroll down to the beach to think about how to put her plans into place. The morning sea breeze felt sweet and fresh against the increasing heat of the sun. In the distance, she could see Renato on his boat. Junior wasn't with him and it dawned on her that the young boy must be at school. She walked towards him and saw that he was busy untangling some ropes.

'Good morning! How are things?'

'Oh, good morning, Ma'am Maya … ' Renato had been caught off guard. He quickly tidied up the ropes and put them aside.

'Are you waiting for some clients to come on board?' Maya asked.

'No, not really. I do hope some will come today, though.'

'Oh, good. Can I get on board then? I want to see the island from the waters. Could you give me a tour?'

Renato's face lit up. He had his first client for the day. 'Yes, of course, Ma'am Maya!' He jumped off the boat to help Maya climb aboard.

Within minutes, the boat was roaring its way from the beach and further into the calm blue sea. Maya sat at the far end, enjoying the beautiful views as the island town faded away from their sight. She thought about asking Renato the questions that had been niggling away at her. He was bound to have his own opinions about the island, too. She moved so she was closer to where he was seated by the steering wheel and took a pew on a bench behind him.

'Are you OK to talk while attending to the steering wheel, Renato?' she shouted over the noise of the boat's engine.

Renato glanced back at her. 'Sure, Ma'am Maya,' he said and lowered the speed of the boat so the engine noise eased.

'Well, I've come to love this island because it's so beautiful, but there's something that bothers me a lot,' Maya started.

'Really, what?'

'Well, I've read about and heard rumours regarding the foreign men, mostly older ones, who flock to this island. What makes you think they want to come here?' Maya hoped that Renato would know the answer.

Renato remained silent and didn't glance back to answer the question. From where she was sat, Maya could see the side of his face suddenly drop. She was puzzled by his silence and wondered whether she had offended him.

It was a few moments later when Renato, half glancing in

Maya's direction, spoke with a solemn voice. 'Ma'am Maya, I've never talked about this to anyone. I've kept it to myself. It happened when I was coming up to 16. I've tried to kill myself many times before, but somehow I've survived. My parents were very naïve. They thought the foreigner – apparently a retired priest – just needed company to tour the island for a small fee. I was pleased to earn a few bucks to help them out. They didn't know that after I had showed the foreigner around, he lured me back to his cottage to watch some movies. Of course, I liked the idea because I'd never had the chance to see a movie before. He had various Betamax tapes in his living room and asked me to choose which one I wanted to watch. Of course, I chose an action movie. He gave me some drinks and snacks while we watched. This happened three times all together, and each time I woke up half naked in bed. He told me I'd fallen asleep while watching the movie and he'd carried me to the spare room.'

They were heading to one of the spots he normally took his passengers to, towards the eastern part of the island. It had a white sandy beach, which looked very serene and pure, and afforded a view of the mainland.

Maya asked Renato to stop by the shore for a while. 'It's OK,' she said gently. 'If you don't want to talk any more about your experience, I completely understand.'

Renato carried on. 'The last time I tried to kill myself, I had to tell my parents the reason. They were devastated and felt extremely guilty. My father, in particular, was so angry and went to the foreigner's cottage with a machete, but by then he'd left the island. Ever since then, I've felt suspicious of every foreigner coming here, especially the white ones. I had to learn how to live with my experience and I took it one day at a time. When I married and had my four children, I promised myself that I would always keep a good eye on them. I won't let what happened to me happen to them.'

The determination showed on Renato's face as he spoke. 'This kind of thing still happens, I think even more so than before. I know some parents whose kids have fallen into the same trap, but I think the elders just try and ignore it, which is very sad. Life is so hard these days. Everyone is trying to make money whenever they can.'

Maya mentioned Keith, and how Junior was with him when she first met them.

'I have known Mr Smith since he arrived on the island last year,' Renato explained. 'As always, I was suspicious of him at first, but I could tell that he was a genuinely nice and helpful person. I trust him. Besides, I was ill at the time. I didn't realise Junior went to the cave with Mr Smith. I am so happy and grateful that you found them and were able to help.' The smile was back on Renato's face.

Relieved over what she had just learned, Maya changed the topic and asked if Renato knew about the waterfall.

'Oh yes, that's my favourite place to unwind and meditate,' he said with enthusiasm. 'I discovered the place with a friend when I was eight. It's very sacred to me and provided solace during my suicidal times. I know some people are scared to even mention it and they consider it a curse, but I think it's a wonderful spot to visit. I believe the deaths that occurred there were accidents – there was nothing mystical about them. I took a few of my clients there on our way back from the cave – they were astonished by its beauty and grateful to me for showing them it.'

Maya was delighted that there was at least one native islander who shared her sentiments about the waterfall, and felt that it was a sacred place rather than a cursed one.

'Do you think the mermaid Lavinia actually existed?' she asked.

Renato tried to contain a chuckle as he replied. 'Some people believe so, but I don't. My grandparents told us many folklore stories when we were kids, but my *lolo* always ended his tales by saying they were only stories. He said that it was up to me whether I believed them or not, and that what we believe becomes a reality. My reality is that I don't believe there is a mermaid in the whirlpool, but nature has its own life and ought to be respected.'

Maya was impressed with Renato's philosophy, as it was so close to her own.

Chapter Eleven

Maya was back at her cottage by lunchtime, but regardless of Renato's positive assessment of Keith, she still had some nagging doubts. Could Keith be one of the paedophiles on the island? How come the officers knew when he left the island? Had he been taken away for investigation? Was he involved in the Karnal paedophile group that apparently roamed Far Eastern countries? She shivered at the thought and tried to shrug it off by preparing her lunch.

She went to the docking port after her meal and noticed that it was unusually quiet for a Monday. She spoke to one of the porters, Berto, whom she regularly gleaned information from. He said it had been quiet all day and that only 10 passengers had arrived on the previous boat, two of whom he was sure were officers.

'What did they look like?' Maya asked. When Berto described them, she thought they might be the ones who had delivered Keith's letter.

She stayed in the waiting area at the dock until the last regular boat trip arrived from the mainland at five. She could count on her fingers the passengers on each one. Some of them were locals who'd gone to do their errands on the mainland. Feeling somewhat disappointed, Maya walked back to her cottage. She wondered where the two officers were staying; maybe they could answer some of her questions about Keith. If only she could meet them again.

Each morning, Maya got up early and walked down to the beach. She bought a map of the island and planned to visit one part of it every day until she had covered all of it. Afterwards, she headed to the docking port to do her regular observing.

Maya gathered her information by talking to locals and tourists. She took notes from those who had resided on the island for a long time, and from those who were just visiting for a holiday. After two weeks of doing hands-on research, she compared her figures to the data that the local tourism department kept. She was amazed to discover that amongst a thousand estimated tourists who had come to the island during that period, there were at least 200 permanent and semi-permanent foreigners. They had been on the island for a number of years; some of them were married or living with local women, with whom they had families. The semi-permanent ones came to stay for a number of months, usually returning for the same period each year. They were from Europe, America, Australia, Canada, New Zealand, Japan and China.

Maya thought what a huge task it would be to gather information on all these foreigners by herself. Some were named in the records – others had only been assigned a number. Her investigative skills began to kick in. She'd forgotten how exciting it was, as it had been a long time since she had covered such an intense topic.

She needed some help and was prepared to share her salary that month with the people who were willing to assist. She recruited some of the locals she knew to get information regarding her 'persons of interest' list. Her helpers included Aida the shopkeeper, Junior's father, Renato, Berto the porter, the ice cream vendor on the beach and the two bartenders from the disco pub. Maya even went to the Beachfront Hotel, which was owned by an Englishman and his *Filipina* wife, Anna Davies. Maya spoke to Anna, who was very accommodating and recounted how she'd met her husband Andy 12 years earlier in Bago City, where she worked in a travel agency. Mr Davies was one of her clients. They got married after two years and honeymooned on the island, which they fell in love with. They decided to move to it permanently and set up their hotel business. This was just when the island was becoming a popular tourist destination outside Manila. They built their business up from a five-bedroom B&B to a huge and opulent five star hotel – the first luxury one on the island. Anna emphasised how it had been perseverance, patience and continuous hard work that had got them to this point and they strived each day to keep up their high standards. Her husband had been a civil engineer and he was very meticulous and knew exactly what he wanted. They had three children together and lived in the penthouse section of the hotel.

Maya thanked Anna for her time and, as she passed by the reception area, she met the hotel supervisor and spoke briefly to her. She learned that Keith was considered a semi-permanent resident, so he had to go on her list.

Chapter Twelve

Maya asked her team to work discreetly, so she could get the information she needed within a week. She knew she could trust them, but the result of their combined effort surprised her. She discovered that most of the people on her list were genuine residents who happened to love the island and were either married to Filipina women and had families and/or had businesses on the island. But 50 of them seemed dodgy, as they didn't have any of these things. If they had partners, then these were women with young families of their own. They didn't seem to have come to the island for the diving or angling either. Keith remained in this section of the list.

Aida told Maya that in their neighbourhood alone there were 15 foreigners, eight of whom lived in the Hilltop

Cottages compound where Maya was staying. She was not particularly surprised at this, as she'd noticed a few of them, especially during her early morning walks to the beach.

'Two of them are staying at the cottages next to each other over there,' said Aida, pointing to the far end of the compound. 'One of them is a Scotsman and the other is Australian. Children come and go regularly.'

The cottage at the end was familiar to Maya. It was the one she'd passed with Keith and heard a woman wailing.

Maya couldn't help herself. She told Aida all about her disturbing experience. Aida looked back at Maya with teary eyes. 'Ma'am Maya, I hate to tell you this, but it happens all the time. The mothers go to these places when they realise what's been happening to their children. They usually plead with the foreigners to stop what they're doing – some even offer themselves to the bastards in return for not touching their kids. My sister Linda was one of them. Maybe it was her you heard that night.'

Aida paused to wipe away her tears with the end of her shirt before continuing. 'The morning after the night you talked about, I found her in her house. She was in a very bad state, almost suicidal. She'd found out her 13-year-old daughter had lost her virginity to that bastard, that animal. He even insisted that the girl was in love with him! Of course she bloody wasn't. What would a girl that age know about love, not to mention with a geriatric like that? He had been luring the child to his cottage behind Linda's back. He'd bought her dresses – sexy dresses – and given her money and chocolates. All the while he was pretending to be in love with my poor little sister! Oh God, forgive me, I wanted to kill him there and then!'

By this point, Aida was sobbing uncontrollably. Maya hugged her. 'I'm very sorry, Aida,' she whispered. But anger was spreading through her own body.

Aida composed herself and looked at Maya with a determined expression. 'I understood at once what you were trying to do when you asked me to help you with this, Ma'am Maya, and I would gladly help you for nothing. I just want this to stop happening on our island. Nobody else has tried to intervene. The authorities seem to be scared, which means we are all scared to talk. You're the only one I know who is brave enough to do this. Please, Ma'am Maya, do your best to stop this. I am getting sick of it, and so are many of the islanders.'

Maya felt sick to her stomach. She couldn't fathom the extent of the paedophilia happening on this beautiful island. She couldn't even bring herself to utter such a despicable word. She was more determined than ever to continue her investigations.'I will do my best, Aida,' she said. 'I can't promise anything, but I will try and expose what's happening.'

She remembered her encounter with Edith at the private resort swimming pool and asked Aida if she knew the kid and her stepfather.

'Yes, I know Edith,' Aida sighed. 'She is one of Betty and Julio's daughters. Sadly, Julio died suddenly three years ago. Betty hooked up with this disgusting old German, whom we all call Herman. He curses every time he speaks.

The rumour is he now controls the lives of Betty and her three girls. Nowadays, I hardly see Betty outside their house. They live in a bungalow next to the resort you went to.'

Maya thanked Aida for her verbal report. As she left for her cottage, Aida added, 'I will be praying for you, Ma'am Maya. Please do take care.' Maya smiled at her and walked up to her cottage.

By the end of the day, she'd managed to speak to everyone in her team. It was hard to figure out how she would validate all the information she'd gathered. A list of 50 was still a long one to work through on her own. On the bright side, no one on her team had spoken negatively about Keith. On the contrary, those who knew him were full of praise and said he was generous, helpful and friendly.

Chapter Thirteen

Maya slept in the following morning and missed her usual early morning walk to the beach. She was only woken by a continuous knock on the door and briefly wondered if it was Aida's nephew, who usually dropped off her Saturday paper. But he didn't normally knock first – he just left it on the chair on the veranda.

Maya was still in her nightie when she opened the door. She was shocked and confused to encounter Keith and was just about to close the door again when he reached out and put his hand on it. 'Please, Maya, may I come in? I really need to talk to you. It's very important. I took the first boat from the mainland this morning. I'm only on the island for the weekend, as I have to go to London on Monday.'

Maya was still confused but hesitantly ushered him in. She went to the kitchen and put the kettle on before grabbing a robe from her bedroom. Keith was sitting in the kitchen when she came out. She made their coffees and sat opposite him, moving the paperwork she'd collated to one side. She'd been so exhausted the night before that she'd forgotten to tidy up.

'First of all, sweetie, I apologise for leaving without seeing you first,' Keith started.

Maya cut him off. 'Don't call me sweetie, I don't know you.'

Keith forced a smile. 'It was very urgent. I …' He hesitated and looked into Maya's eyes. He knew his job was in jeopardy if he divulged it to just anyone, but Maya was different, his instinct had told him that he could trust her from the moment he met her. 'Please, this is just between you and me … I am not just a photographer, I also work for the ISAF – the International Secret Agent Force, if you've heard of it. Our head office is in London.'

Maya shook her head and looked at Keith in bewilderment.

'I've been a secret agent since I left the Royal Air Force,' he continued. 'I was assigned to South Africa before the Queen's Commonwealth tour to assess the security for her and her entourage. I loved it there and decided to apply for a post in the country, but then an agent was needed in the area indefinitely …' Keith paused to sip his coffee before carrying on. 'Agents could be assigned anywhere in the world to assess the security for highly important people, such as royal families, presidents, religious leaders and other world dignitaries. However, I'm here now for a totally different reason. This is the first time our force has taken up an assignment like this.

'A growing group of men and women are sexually abusing children around the world. The paedophile ring is called Karnal and it's very powerful and growing rapidly. After a thorough intelligence surveillance, it was discovered that their main centre is here on the island.'

Maya realised her suspicion about Keith was baseless and a lot of her questions regarding him had been answered. The brief article she'd read in the *SunStar* now made more sense. She felt guilty for doubting him and her admiration began to grow again.

Keith explained that he'd had to leave that day at dawn because he and his team, which included the two officers who'd given Maya his letter, had realised that one of their 'most wanted' had escaped the previous night on a private boat. Keith tried to trace him in Manila, but it was too late – the man had already boarded a plane to Bangkok. Keith followed him there and finally collared him with the help of intelligence forces in Thailand. The man was now in custody awaiting trial.

'I'm very sorry,' Maya mumbled.

'For what?'

'For doubting you,' she said meekly and lowered her gaze to the table.

'No, don't be. It was my fault. I should have told you about myself sooner.'

Keith reached out across the table and grabbed Maya's hand. 'I knew you were special from the moment I met you. I don't want to hurt or lose you.'

When Maya raised her eyes, she saw in Keith's his

sincerity and love. She felt butterflies suddenly churn in her stomach and quickly changed the subject of their conversation. 'I read something about a paedophile ring on this island a few weeks ago and, to cut a long story short, I've been doing my own investigation.' She reached for her paperwork and brought out her 'final 50' list.

Keith nodded and smiled. 'I noticed your list when you went to get your robe and had a quick peek at it. I must say, you're very clever.'

He moved his chair next to Maya's and read through the list, ticking off all the names with a pen. 'These people are all on our watch list, and there's more.'

'Oh, I have another list,' said Maya. 'I had two hundred initially and we've scaled it down to what I call the "dodgy ones."'

'"We?" he asked, as he glanced through Maya's alternative list.

'Oh yes, I have my own team of trusted local investigators too,' she proudly declared.

Keith winked at her briefly before scrutinising the list further. He ticked off 30 more names.

'At the moment, we have 80 on our watch list,' he said. 'Listen, do you realise how dangerous this is? These people are very powerful and discreet. Trying to catch them can be tricky. They use everything and every person they can to disguise their real intentions. Politics and corruption also come into play. Do you understand what I mean?'

'Yes, I realise that,' Maya replied. 'But I have been naive for many months. I didn't see this coming and I want to help the best way I can. I owe it to the local people here and the children. I know I have their full backing.'

Keith put his arms around her shoulders and she didn't shrug them off. Instead, she leant her head on his muscular chest. The flutters in her stomach started again. Keith turned her face round to his and kissed her, gently at first and then passionately, as Maya responded unreservedly.

'I love you and I missed you so much,' Keith declared as they disengaged from their moment of passion.

'I missed you very much, too. Since you left I've changed my routine and I've been going to the docking port every day, with the hope of seeing you again.' She leant her head on his chest again, feeling a strong sense of security there.

Moments later, they walked out to the veranda together and sat quietly on the chairs, their arms entwined. They watched the sun rising, and its reflection made the blue sea appear white.

'I love this spot,' said Keith. 'I'd like nothing more than to sit here and watch the day go by, but I have to go to the hotel and start packing.'

Maya didn't move. She wished she could forever lean her tiny head against Keith's wide, strong chest. She felt secure there and her problems vanished into thin air. Suddenly, she felt a pang of sadness as she realised he would soon be going away again.

Keith stroked her hair and held her tight. 'We will work this out, my sweetie, I promise.' He moved Maya around to face him. Tears had started to fall down her cheeks and

Keith gently wiped them away. 'Don't cry, my love. This will work out, I am sure of it. We just need to be strong.'

Maya nodded and stood up.

'I have to leave and take the first boat on Monday morning,' Keith continued. 'My flight to London is in the evening, but I have things to attend to at our Manila quarters during the day. I don't know how long I'll be away, but my bosses urgently need me to be there to discuss other strategies. I hope it'll only be for a couple of weeks, but it could be months. I'll leave you my sister's phone number in case you need to contact me. I will be staying at her house just outside the city.'

As Keith stood up, he asked, 'Do you want to come over to the hotel for dinner tonight?' Then he added with a smile, 'or can I come here and you can cook?'

'I'll come to the hotel,' Maya replied. She didn't know what she would make for their dinner. She hadn't been prepared for Keith's appearance that morning. He kissed her again before leaving for the hotel.

Chapter Fourteen

Maya remained on the veranda wondering what had just happened. It was surreal. The day before, she'd been sure Keith was a paedophile and that she would forever hate him. Now he'd answered her nagging questions without her having to ask. And he'd kissed her like no other man had kissed her before. She felt her stomach churn again at the thought of his passionate embrace. At this point, she was sure that 'like' wasn't the right word to describe her feelings. She was in love!

It was six o'clock by the time she got to the hotel. When she got off the tricycle, Keith was outside waiting for her. They dined at the restaurant again and Maya enjoyed her seafood meal. She offered to pay the bill, but Keith said that the hotel would charge it to his work. He invited Maya to his hotel room and she accepted. She was curious about what the rooms looked like. Keith's was on the top floor and was the only other penthouse apart from the owners' family residence.

Mr Davies and Keith were good friends, as they'd gone to the same high school in England. They'd lost touch after going to university and moving on with their careers, and it was a sweet coincidence that they'd met again on the island after all those years.

Maya was awestruck by the elegance of Keith's penthouse. She'd stayed in many hotels before for work, but none compared to this. No wonder it had such a prestigious reputation and was well respected by everyone on the island.

Keith was amused by Maya's almost child-like reaction to his living quarters. She couldn't contain her joy as she moved around, checking out every corner. Past the kitchenette there was even a little terrace with a 190-degree view of the island and sea. Keith had set up a large telescope in the corner.

Apart from his daughter, there was no one in Keith's life who made him feel he was capable of so much love. Maya was clever as well as beautiful. She had this determination that most men would admire.

There was only one thing that puzzled Keith. Maya seemed to be supressing something. He realised that apart from her being a journalist, he hardly knew anything about her background. However, he was sure she was the girl he'd been waiting for all these years. He was determined to make their relationship work.

Maya walked into the bedroom and noticed Keith's two sets of luggage in the corner. She went straight over to the enormous window overlooking the sea. It had a very good view of the beach where she often took her walks, and the disco pub where they'd met for a second time.

The fading sunset was as beautiful as ever. Maya never tired of watching and admiring it, as it reminded her of the beauty and mystery of life. That night she thought it looked extra special because she was in this special place, with a special someone by her side. She smiled with contentment.

Keith watched Maya's every move. Her tiny black dress clung tightly to her every curve; a sight that made his heart beat faster than usual. No one else made him feel such strong, loving emotions.

Keith wondered what had happened to the old him, the man who had trained for many years to be constantly on guard and to never show his emotions. Maybe his age was catching up with him and putting him more in touch with his soul. Whatever it was, he loved the new him.

Keith stood behind Maya as she looked out of the window and wrapped his strong arms around her tiny waist. 'You look stunning and irresistible, my sweetness,' he whispered.

Maya felt the familiar flutters in her stomach again. Keith gently moved her long, black hair to one side and began to kiss the nape of her neck. Maya thought she would melt. She couldn't remember feeling like this before with Arthur, who was the only other person she'd had a proper relationship with.

Keith continued to kiss Maya's neck as he ran his large

hands along her upper thigh and up to her chest, before cupping her breasts. Maya couldn't control the noise she was making from the pleasurable sensations she was feeling. Keith went on to kiss her chest and face all over until finally locating her lips. They remained locked in a passionate kiss for a few minutes and Maya felt she was drowning in pleasure.

They pulled apart to quickly undress each other and then Keith gently carried Maya to his massive bed. They kissed, caressed and wrestled each other while making unbridled howling noises. Then Keith entered her and after a few moments all she could feel was the most pleasurable experience in the world. She screamed and Keith let her relax for a bit before continuing to thrust until he came.

Exhausted and satisfied, Keith cuddled Maya and whispered, 'That was wonderful, my sweetness.'

'I've never felt something like that before,' Maya replied. She smiled and buried her head in Keith's naked chest, her favourite spot. He was wearing aftershave and smelled very masculine.

Maya was suddenly thirsty and Keith got up to get her a glass of water, pouring one for himself at the same time. He climbed back into bed and Maya clung on to him. 'Please don't leave me, Keith, promise,' she whispered.

'No, definitely not! I promise we will work this out. I want you in my life forever.' He wrapped his strong arms around her once again.

Maya began to relay her life story to Keith … the tragic deaths of her parents, her adopted family, her education and her career. She told him in detail about Arthur, his infidelity and how she was infertile.

'I thought for a long time that I didn't have a meaningful purpose in life except to do well in my career,' Maya said. 'That was until now. I want to be with you forever, too, but I'm also scared I will lose you.' She sobbed and hid her face in his chest.

Keith was humbled by Maya's honesty. It was now clear to him why she'd avoided talking about her life. She had been through so much and Keith was even more determined to protect and take care of her.

'I promise you, my love, it will happen. We will be together forever.'

He took Maya's hands, kissed them and lifted them to his chest. 'Feel my heart,' he said. Maya smiled as she felt the beat inside.

They talked more about their goals and aspirations and shared some silly stuff, too, which they giggled and laughed about like children. Maya confessed that she wasn't a good cook and Keith joked that she should start learning. It was midnight by the time they fell asleep while holding each other.

The following morning, Keith asked Maya if she had something planned and when she said she hadn't he suggested hiring Renato's boat and going for a picnic. He thought Renato would know the best spot and Maya agreed.

They had their breakfast at the hotel restaurant and then Keith walked Maya outside to hail a tricycle. Keith spoke to the girl behind reception and asked her to book their boat ride and picnic with Renato. Keith and Maya would meet him at the usual place on the beach before midday. The receptionist reassured him that his message would be delivered.

After Maya had left, Keith went up to his room and continued packing. He didn't know how long he would be away and the hotel might want to book out the penthouse. He disassembled the telescope on the terrace and put it in its box. A lot of his stuff was to do with his photography and the rest concerned his investigations. He packed everything up in half a dozen boxes and put them in Mr Davies' storage room, which had been previously agreed. He only had to take two sets of luggage with him to London.

Chapter Fifteen

Renato was waiting at the beach when Keith and Maya arrived for their picnic. As it was Sunday, Junior was able to accompany them. He told Keith and Maya how happy he was to see the two of them together. Keith smiled and winked at him while Maya gave him a hug. Strangely, she saw him like a little brother. She had so much respect for this family, especially Renato. He'd been through a lot in his younger years and Maya could see how much he cared for his children and how protective of them he was. She wondered if he would ever tell them what had happened to him when he was a teenager.

Maya said hello to Renato and he smiled back and nodded. She'd spoken to him the previous Friday about his report and he was very pleased to help with the cause. Like Aida and the rest of her team, he didn't want anything from

Maya in exchange for his information, but Maya insisted on giving them all a payment.

Renato started the boat and they tootled along for 20 minutes before stopping at an amazing alcove of rocky beaches. There wasn't another soul in sight – they had found their rocky paradise!

Maya was in awe.

'I told you this man was a gem,' Keith said to her. 'He knows this island like the back of his hand.'

Maya repeatedly nodded in approval.

Renato found a safe spot for them to disembark. Keith helped Maya get off the boat and they walked together along the rocky beach, happy to explore the area.

Junior unloaded the picnic boxes and brought out their supply of bottled water and soft drinks. To keep them cool, he submerged them in a rock pool. He carried the rest of the boxes to a little camping area under a large tree and then went off towards the bushes to gather firewood.

Meanwhile, Renato set up the picnic mats. He prepared a firewood stove made up of three rocks arranged in a triangle, and, when Junior came back with the wood, he started a fire. He put some rice into a pot and covered it with water before placing it on top of the stove to cook. Father and son clearly knew their jobs.

Keith and Maya continued to navigate the beach, heading for the big rock that marked the curve of the alcove. Each time they passed a rock pool, they investigated it and, like children, they tried to outdo each other by naming the little creatures that inhabited it. There were sea anemones, brown seaweed, crabs, green algae, whelks, limpets, snails, shrimps and some other strange looking things that they agreed to call 'unidentified creatures'. Keith had his camera with him, as always, and took lots of photos so he could eventually try to identify them.

By the time they reached the curved point of the alcove, they could hear Junior calling them from afar. He said that he and his father were going to check the fishing net they'd put out earlier and would be back in half an hour or so.

'OK, Junior, see you both soon,' Keith called back.

The couple waved as they watched Renato and Junior roar out to sea on the boat. The weather was glorious, the sky was blue and the temperature had peaked. Thank goodness they were both wearing their caps, sunglasses, vests, shorts and walking sandals.

They continued with their adventure. The big rock was easy enough to climb onto. The scenery was so beautiful that Keith kept taking photos. They sat there for a while, arms entwined as they soaked up the beauty of nature. They talked about how lucky they were to be able to explore such extraordinarily beautiful spots.

'A perfect paradise island,' declared Maya.

Realising what she had just said, she looked at Keith and their eyes met. They both shook their heads.

'I take that back,' Maya corrected herself. 'Sadly, this won't be a perfect island until the problem is solved.'

They made their way to the camp by the large tree and were glad to have the shade. They were both sweating, but as they lay down on the picnic blanket they could feel the delightful sea breeze drying off their skin. Maya went to get some of the drinks from the rock pool. The bottled water and cola felt like it had come straight from the fridge. She noticed the stove and went to check on it. The rice was cooked.

'Father and son are the perfect match for their business, eh?' she said to Keith. 'They know exactly what they're doing. I'm so impressed. Renato has trained Junior well.'

'That's true,' Keith replied, relishing the taste of his cool cola.

As they relaxed, Keith dozed off. Maya left him to rest and went off to gather some wild raspberries, which she'd spotted in the bushes 10 metres away. She came back with her hat full of wild fruit. Keith woke when she joined him back on the mat.

'Whoops, I didn't mean to sleep,' he laughed. 'It's unbelievably relaxing here.' His eyes widened when Maya showed him the contents of her hat.

'You must have needed a little rest. Here, try some,' she offered.

'Wow, they look delicious! Where did you get them and what are they? They look like raspberries, only much larger.'

'They are wild raspberries,' Maya explained. 'We call them "sapinit". There are so many that I couldn't stop picking them. When I was a kid I used to gather them in the fields of our farm. My father showed me where they were.'

Keith picked one up and ate it, then another and another. 'Mmmm, they're sweet and sour at the same time. I like them a lot. Unlike strawberries, they have nothing much inside and they just melt in your mouth.'

They had nearly finished the berries when they heard the roar of Renato's boat. Junior was waving and looked happy as he approached the beach. Keith and Maya walked towards the boat.

'We had a real good catch,' Junior shouted.

They disembarked and Renato brought out a large Styrofoam cooler box and opened it in front of Keith and Maya.

'Wow, that's a lot!' Maya exclaimed, as she examined the contents of the box. There were a couple of big lobsters, some large crabs, milkfish, carp, king prawns and a few little fish. Junior had a plastic tub of fresh seaweed too.

'There are many more in the boat, *Ate*,' Junior giggled. 'These are just for us to cook here.'

'Sorry, it took us a bit longer than we anticipated. Are you really hungry now?' Renato asked.

'No, we're fine, don't worry,' Keith replied. 'Besides, we've just had some of Maya's wild berry pickings.'

'Ah, so you've had *sapinits* already,' Junior remarked. 'I was going to pick some for you later.'

'Yes, I spotted them over there. I enjoyed picking them even though the bushes were so thorny!' Maya laughed.

'We'll cook these now, it won't be long until our lunch,' Renato said, carrying the box towards the makeshift cooking area with Junior in tow.

'Do you fancy a swim?' Keith asked Maya.

'Sure.'

They walked towards a spot far enough away to be out

of sight of the father and son duo. They took off their shirts and shorts and got into the water. The temperature felt good against the heat of the early afternoon sun. They frolicked and swam, giggled and kissed.

'You look totally irresistible and sexy with your long wet hair,' Keith teased Maya, giving her a lingering and passionate kiss.

By the time they walked back to their makeshift camp hand in hand, there was a spread of seafood ready for them on the picnic mat, including steamed lobster, crabs, prawns and a variety of barbequed fish. To accompany the fish feast were vegetables, rice and a spicy salad made from seaweed, tomatoes and onions. Their cool drinks were waiting for them on the side too. Renato and Junior were seated at the far end by the cooking area. Maya called out for them to join her and Keith.

'It's OK, Ma'am Maya, we'll have ours here. We hope you both enjoy yours.'

Maya looked at Keith and he walked over to Renato and Junior. 'We want you both to come and eat with us, please,' he said.

'OK, Mr Smith,' Renato replied and picked up their plates and food.

They enjoyed a good meal together and joked and laughed all the way through it. Junior was more talkative and jolly than his father and wasn't at all shy, which was in contrast to when Maya first met him. He quizzed Keith about his life as a child and Keith obliged with stories of his adventures. He recalled being a young boy in the Highlands of Scotland.

Before his family moved to England they had a little farm and herded a number of sheep. He also went fishing with his father.

'It's nothing like this, though,' he said. 'It was mostly cold there and it often snowed heavily during the winter. I had more heavy and thick clothes than shorts and vests.' He went on to explain that his family – his father, mother and younger sister, Katriona – moved to England when he was 10. His father fell ill, which meant he was no longer strong enough to tend to their farm and they had to sell it. They moved to Yorkshire and his father got a job as a primary school janitor while his mother became a child minder.

'What do you want to do when you're older?' Keith asked Junior.

'Oh, I'm going to be a policeman,' he stated without hesitation, which made them all laugh.

'Wow, that's a good profession,' said Keith, patting Junior's shoulders. 'Carry on with it and you will do well.' In response, Junior smiled proudly.

'I hope my children will become what they want to be in the future,' said Renato. 'I try to instil in them the way of life here on the island. I want them to always be conscientious and resourceful, and to use nature so that they can live no matter what happens to their dreams.'

Maya nodded in agreement and was glad that Renato was becoming more vocal.

By the time they finished eating, there was hardly anything left of the spread.

'That was totally delicious!' said Maya. 'I've never had a picnic with so much variety of scrumptious food.'

'Me too,' Keith agreed. 'Thank you very much, Renato and Junior.'

'You're welcome. I'm glad you both enjoyed it,' Renato replied as he and Junior cleared the picnic mat. Maya tried to help tidy up but Renato insisted there was no need. He suggested that she and Keith should just rest and relax.

As they reclined on the mat, Keith held Maya in his arms and played briefly with her long hair. They sat quietly for a while, feeling the sea breeze on their faces and enjoying the tranquillity of their wonderful spot. Eventually, they both dozed off and slept for the next half an hour.

When they woke up, Renato was busy loading their picnic stuff onto the boat while Junior dived from a rock and took a swim. Keith and Maya stood up and stretched their legs.

'Come and join me?' Junior called out. Keith decided to test his diving skills while Maya chose to watch.

It was only then that she had a good look at Keith's physical attributes. Considering his age, he had an athletic body and Maya smiled at the thought that he was 10 years older than her – he certainly didn't look his age. He was six foot and probably weighed around sixteen stone. His hair was shaven and he had attractive blue eyes.

Maya had never considered physical appearance as the basis of love. It was good character and a positive attitude that attracted her most. But it just so happened that Keith possessed these attributes as well as being so masculine and attractive. He looked very sexy in his trunks as he dived after Junior. Maya watched them fondly as they repeatedly dived from the rock with forward, backward, reverse and twisting styles. They were clearly enjoying themselves.

When they got out of the water, Keith gasped when he reached Maya. 'I'm so knackered,' he said, reaching for his vest and shorts. 'I'd forgotten how much fun it is to dive. I'm glad I did it.'

Maya smiled at him adoringly. 'I can't dive but I loved watching you both. You were so good and natural, and sexy too.' She winked and Keith gave her a brief peck on the lips.

It was coming up to five in the afternoon when they boarded Renato's boat and headed back to the island town. On their way, Maya asked Junior how he had learned to dive. He happily recounted how his father had taught him how to swim in the sea back when he barely knew how to walk. As he grew, he gradually learned more. Whenever he had the chance he watched the island's professional divers and hoped someday he would be able to wear all their interesting diving gear and make full use of the equipment.

'Very good,' Maya said to him. Her admiration for this little boy grew each time she saw him. He wasn't only clever, but he was very positive about life too. This clearly reflected how far Renato had come in dealing with his own miserable childhood experiences. He had made sure that his own children, his son in particular, had a brighter outlook on life.

When they disembarked the boat close to the beach, Maya declared, 'I've really enjoyed myself. It's been the best day out I've had in a long time. Thank you ever so much.' She hugged Junior and shook Renato's hands.

Keith reached inside his pocket and handed some money to Renato. 'I don't want any change,' he said.

Renato shook his head. 'This is far too much, Mr Smith.' He tried to give some of the money back but Keith gently pushed Renato's hand back and then shook it firmly instead. 'Today has been priceless. I can't thank you enough.'

'It has been my joy to make you all happy and contented,' Renato replied. 'Thank you very much for your generosity.'

Keith nodded before turning to Junior and shaking his hand. 'Thanks, my little diving instructor,' he joked, before briefly rubbing his head.

'You're very welcome, Mr Smith and *Ate* Maya, we had a great time with you both too. Thank you and see you both around again soon. We're heading off to the Beachfront Hotel to deliver the rest of our catch.'

After saying goodbye to the duo, Keith and Maya walked up the hill to Maya's cottage. They'd agreed that Maya would stay at the hotel that night and as she got changed inside, Keith lazed in the hammock on the veranda. Maya packed a bag and they both headed back to the hotel along the beach.

Chapter Sixteen

That evening, they dined at the hotel restaurant once more, but this time they both opted for a chicken dish. When they returned to his room, Keith finished his packing. He reminded Maya that she had his sister's number if she needed to reach him and she remembered her pager, which she only used to beep her editor whenever her articles were on their way to him. She scribbled the number down for Keith. Telecommunication services were under development in remote areas of the country, especially the islands, so a telephone connection was rare outside the tourism department and a few of the hotels. Keith said that if he had a message to pass on to Maya he would also try to contact the Beachfront Hotel. He warned her to be extra careful with her own investigative journalism.

They went to bed early, making love before they fell asleep and again when they woke in the morning. They repeatedly declared their love for each other and vowed to try and remain strong while they were temporarily apart.

In the morning, Keith took the first boat to the mainland and Maya was tearful as she bade him goodbye. Keith felt a pang of sadness inside too.

Maya tried hard to concentrate on other things and avoided thinking and worrying about Keith. She finalised her 'persons of interest' list, which, thanks to her lover's information, now stood at 80. She kept herself busy, discreetly visiting the areas where the suspicious foreigners lived. She pretended to be a tour operator from Manila and said she had been assigned there for a few months to look for the most interesting tourist spots on the island. It took her two weeks to complete her investigation.

Maya could understand what Keith had said about how tricky it was to pin these people down. It was hard to get evidence, as those close to the questionable foreigners kept quiet. However, most of the locals Maya spoke to told her about the disgusting lives they led. The locals tolerated them because of the economic benefits they brought, which the politicians were quick to remind them about.

Maya sent her usual articles for the following four weeks. In the fourth one, she made a separate note for Tito Eddy about the alleged paedophile ring on the island. She added that she was looking into it. As usual, she sent him a beeper message as soon as she posted them out. She thought it was unusual that she didn't receive a reply. He always sent her one line with something like, 'good job, girl', 'brilliant' or 'thanks'. Maya assumed that he must be very busy.

The following Thursday morning, Maya received a pager message from Gina.

> Just to let you know, the new Chief Editor and two of his staff are on their way to the island this morning.

Maya was puzzled. New Chief Editor? What had happened to Tito Eddy? Ah, no wonder he hadn't replied …

At mid afternoon, three men turned up at Maya's cottage. She let them in and ushered them to the living room. They told her how they were from *The Pinoy News*. The youngest looking of the three spoke first. 'I am Jose Reyes, the new Chief Editor of PN,' he explained. 'With me are Gerome and Dante, my assistants. I'm sorry if we didn't give you enough notice about our arrival.'

Maya noted that his tone suggested he wasn't sorry at all. She knew better than to mention that Gina had forewarned her. She was shocked to see how young the new Chief Editor was. She guessed he was just a few years older than her. Maybe 36. She took an instant dislike to him. He had an air of suffocating arrogance about him and she'd been expecting someone who was at least the same age as Tito Eddy, who was in his sixties.

'No problem, sir,' she managed to say. 'I didn't know Tito Eddy had been replaced.' She looked at the other two guys, whom she didn't recognise.

'Well,' Jose Reyes said as he slouched on the chair. 'There have been many changes within the company since the takeover last year. Don't ask me about all of them because I'm new here, too. I heard that there was a reshuffle and some resigned and others applied for early retirement. Tito Eddy opted for retirement and finished his job last week.'

He paused and looked at Maya with a hint of a grin on his face. 'The thing is, Maya, included in these changes is your role. We no longer need you here on the island. We are cutting costs and want you back at head office next week.'

Maya was totally shaken by this news. She stared at Jose Reyes before turning to the other two men, who both nodded.

'Wh … why? My contract was for a year and I'm only on my tenth month. There are only two months to go. Can't I finish it?'

'I'm afraid not. Your contract is at the discretion of the management and they have made a decision … it will have to finish earlier.'

Jose Reyes dismissed her plea and went on to tell her that she had to leave the cottage by the weekend.

'If you need any help, we're staying on the island tonight, at the Western Hotel.'

'No thank you,' Maya said as the men got up to leave. Inside she was thinking, 'damn you!'

After the men had gone, Maya slumped on the sofa. She was confused, angry and felt so helpless. She wasn't ready to leave the island just yet … far from it. She hadn't even finalised her investigation. She recalled how she had sent a note to Tito Eddy about the issue she was looking into. She suddenly became scared that someone else had read it and wondered if this was the reason for her early departure.

She stood up and started pacing the living room floor. 'Oh my God,' she mumbled. 'What have I done? And what do I do now?'

She went to the kitchen and drank some water to try and calm herself. She was shaking as she sat down in the kitchen. 'If only Keith were here,' she thought. She realised it was over four weeks since he'd left for London and she'd not heard from him since.

Maya remained seated and rested her head on the table top. She had to remain calm and think straight. There was no need to panic or get scared. She needed to make a plan. Eventually, she got up and went to sit on the veranda.

'It's nearly sunset and then another new day will dawn,' she sighed. Her mind was racing with what ifs and if onlys. She took three deep breaths and finally started to relax.

As she stood up to go inside, a man passed by the little path outside her cottage and smiled at her before continuing on his way.

Maya made her dinner and went to eat outside while the sun went down. She thought about Keith and how she missed him more this time. But she had to be strong — that was their deal.

By the time she went back inside, she knew what she had to do. She felt like a new woman, with a new purpose. There would be a new dawn in her life. She smiled at the thought.

She started packing her things, carrying on through the evening until she had almost filled her three suitcases. She made sure her investigative notes were well hidden away. That was very important to her. She could use them to write anywhere; she didn't have to be on the island to compile the article she had in mind. She decided that she would be in Manila by the following night.

It was nearly midnight when she managed to get to bed and she fell asleep straight away. It had been a long and eventful day.

Chapter Seventeen

The following morning, Maya took a tricycle to the Beachfront Hotel. She asked the receptionist if it was possible to use their telephone to call Keith. She nodded and called someone through an intercom. After five minutes, Anna Davies emerged from the lift with a smile on her face. 'Good morning, Maya, it's good to see you. How are you?'

Maya shook her head, about to cry. Anna motioned her to follow and they went up to her penthouse apartment, where she offered Maya a drink. The place was very quiet; Anna told Maya that the kids were at school and her husband was out on his morning round of meticulous room checks. They had coffee and sat on the sofa in the living room. Maya couldn't help but admire the elegance of the place, which was a larger version of Keith's old suite.

'Maya, I was going to send one of our workers to get

you to come here. Keith phoned last night and spoke to my husband.'

Maya almost jumped from her seat. Anna told her to calm down. 'He is fine. He asked us to tell you that he has to stay in London a little bit longer, but the mission is almost finished.'

Maya scrutinised Anna's face as she tried to work out what the message was all about.

'The line was not particularly clear,' Anna continued. 'But my hubby said that Keith repeatedly asked him to tell you that the mission is almost complete. And that he misses you.'

Relief flooded through her. 'Thank you so much for the message, Anna, and to Mr Davies too. I feel so much better knowing that Keith still remembers me! The thing is though, Anna, I am leaving for Manila this afternoon and I need to talk to Keith or send him a message. I wanted to ask if I could use your telephone?'

'Of course, you can use it from here. We have the main line and the extension at reception. May I ask why you're leaving and when are you coming back?' The concern was evident on Anna's face.

Maya recounted the details of what had happened the day before. By the end of her description, she couldn't control her sobbing. Anna hugged her and tried to reassure her that everything was going to be OK. She encouraged her to do what she thought was best for her and to take each day at a time.

They tried several times to contact the number that Keith

had left for Maya. When they finally got through, it was an answering machine. Maya hesitated, as she did not like leaving messages.

When she finally spoke, she said, 'Hi, good morning. I hope this is the phone number of Katriona Brown, the sister of Keith Smith. If so, I would like to leave a message for him, please. If not, just disregard it. My name is Maya Wara … '

She hesitated for a moment, but Anna encouraged her to carry on. 'I am his friend in Puerto Galla. Can you please tell him that I have to leave the island this afternoon. I'm being sent back to our head office in Manila for good. Please tell him that I think it has to do with my investigation. I got his message from last night. Please also let him know that I am fine and that I miss him. Thank you very much.'

Maya put the phone down and stared at it for a while. She was glad to have somehow made a connection with Keith. She smiled at Anna and thanked her for her help.

'My pleasure,' Anna replied. She wished Maya well and told her she was always welcome to stay at the hotel should she return to the island. They hugged and Maya made her way out. She remembered how Renato usually came to the hotel to make his deliveries and she went back to reception to leave a message for him and Junior. She said she was leaving the island so she wouldn't see them for a while.

On her way back to the cottage, Maya visited Aida's shop.

'I wanted to stop by briefly to say goodbye, my friend,' she said, trying to avoid Aida's shocked gaze.

'Wh … what do you mean, Ma'am Maya?'

'Well, I have to leave the island today, Aida. I don't really want to, but my job here was unexpectedly cut short and I need to go back to our head office in Manila.'

'Oh, what a shame, Ma'am Maya. I'll surely miss you. Well, I'm gutted. But what about the report we've been working on? Please, Ma'am, don't forget to give us a voice, the silent islanders.'

Maya hugged her. 'I'll do my very best, my dear friend,' she said.

After ensuring that all her belongings were packed and the cottage was left tidy, she took some coins and notes from her wallet and left them on the kitchen table with a note thanking the cleaner. She left the keys in the door before looking out at the view from the veranda for one last time.

She took a tricycle to the docking port. The porter, Berto, was there to help her with her suitcases and he said how sad he was to see her go. She took the mid-afternoon boat to the mainland, barely looking back as it left the port. She could barely control the tears that were hidden behind her sunglasses. She had not wanted to leave the island this way.

'Goodbye for now, my beloved island,' she said softly. Thanks for changing my life.' As she spoke, a gust of wind swept past her face and across the half-empty passenger boat.

Chapter Eighteen

It was early Friday evening when Maya arrived at the bus terminal in Manila. Brenda's husband, Alex, came to pick her up.

As soon as she'd got off the boat on the mainland, Maya had phoned Brenda using the public telephone booth. Brenda was surprised to hear of her friend's sudden departure and was worried about her. They were childhood friends and practically knew every detail of each other's lives. Brenda considered Maya her younger sister and would do anything for her. She offered her a place to stay at their home in Manila.

Brenda and Alex lived in a two-bedroom apartment with their two young children, Mandy, five, and three-year-old Noah. Brenda insisted the kids could stay with them in their bedroom to give Maya some privacy, and she reluctantly agreed. She could have stayed in a hotel but she was desperate to talk to her best friend.

That night they had a tearful but wonderful reunion dinner. Maya was godmother to Mandy and the two played together and bonded for half an hour before Alex took the kids to bed.

The two best friends spent the rest of the evening catching up after a long ten months apart. Brenda was most excited to hear about Maya's new love. She was very happy for her and repeatedly said Maya deserved a fresh start. It was coming up to midnight when they both went to sleep.

Maya needed to arrange some more permanent accommodation in Manila. The tenant's contract in her own apartment had two months remaining, so she would have to look for alternative accommodation until then. She couldn't stay with Brenda's family for long, as they needed their space too.

The following day, Maya met up with Gina for lunch at a nearby mall. It was Saturday and the food court was buzzing. Maya had forgotten how it felt to be in a city, as she was so used to the quietness and tranquillity of the island. She felt overwhelmed, suffocated and very uncomfortable. They decided to go to a quieter restaurant instead.

Gina offered Maya the spare room in her apartment until

she could move back into her own. Gina was single but after a few failed relationships was currently dating David, an engineer for a telephone company. He was constantly being assigned to different areas of the country, so Gina was mostly by herself. When Maya quizzed her about this, Gina casually said he was kind of a boyfriend but they weren't serious. They only met when it suited them. She laughed when she noticed Maya's questioning look. 'Oh Maya, my dear, I'm not ready for a serious relationship yet. I enjoy my career and I want to achieve more. I have no time for commitment and I definitely don't want to get tied up with raising kids at this point. I am only 24 for goodness sake! It might be another decade before I start a family, that is, if I decide to have one.'

Maya couldn't help but admire her colleague's tenacity. 'Good idea, I couldn't agree more,' she said.

They agreed that Maya could move into Gina's apartment the following day.

Gina updated Maya on the changes at their workplace. 'I must warn you that it's a mess at the moment.'

'In what way?'

'Well, many colleagues have resisted the changes to management, as most of them are loyal to Tito Eddy. As a result, they are also leaving or taking early retirement. And you know what? The new proprietor is an oligarch and a good friend of the owners of the Western Hotel. That's the hotel where the new Chief Editor stayed when he came to see you on the island, remember?'

Maya's stunned face was a mirror of revelation. 'Aha,

that explains why they wanted me out of there as soon as possible.'

Gina nodded.

The three co-owners of the Western Hotel in Puerto Galla were from America, Canada and China. What's more, they were all on Maya's original 'persons of interest' list. The American and the Canadian had Filipina partners who had young children from their previous relationships. The Chinese man was married to a Filipina but they didn't have kids and he was constantly travelling back and forth to the island. The business was registered under the names of the women because under Philippine law foreigners couldn't fully own businesses in the country. The three men were also amongst the ones that Keith had added to Maya's list of 50 dodgy characters. It was becoming clear why Maya had been pulled from the island and she was more determined than ever to expose what was happening.

Most of Maya's close former colleagues had either been sacked or had left the company. Gina's department had not been affected so far and she had alternatives if the management ever changed her role. She had contacts with other newspaper companies and a television station had offered her a job, which she could take up any time. However, she loved being a field reporter and was not yet ready to move.

Maya was particularly upset about her former editor Tito Eddy's apparent early retirement. That evening, she met up with him at his house. Maya knew his family and had enjoyed dinner with them countless times. They treated her as one of their own and Maya regarded Tito Eddy as a father figure and his wife *Tita* Elena as a loveable aunt. She always asked for Tito Eddy's advice, not only about work but life in general. He'd been especially helpful during her tumultuous relationship with Arthur. Tito Eddy had always believed in Maya, which is why he had recruited her shortly after her graduation and supported her throughout her career with the company. He'd also been the driving force behind her relocation to Puerto Galla.

Tito Eddy was a very gentle and softly spoken man and Maya had never heard him raise his voice at work, even during the most tense and pressurised times. This was why everyone respected his leadership. He had very high principles in life and wouldn't compromise over anything untoward.

Over a scrumptious dinner with the couple, Tito Eddy revealed something that caught Maya off-guard. 'So, you've finally uncovered the rumour, then. I knew you would do it!'

'Tito … you knew all about the thing?' Maya asked, looking at her former boss with wide eyes. Tita Elena was seated across the table from Maya. She smiled but remained silent.

'Of course, my girl. That was the main reason I sent you to the island.' Tito Eddy grinned as he looked between his wife and Maya. 'Your articles with your special note arrived the week I left the office. Grace, my ever-faithful secretary read it and phoned me straight away. I no longer had the beeper, so I couldn't message you.'

Maya remained tongue-tied for a few seconds, 'Oh, I see,' she finally said, smiling at her most respected mentor. 'Thank you, Tito, for entrusting me with such a sensitive and important issue. It certainly was a big challenge, but very worth it!'

After dinner, Tita Elena said goodnight and left Maya and Tito Eddy in the living room, where they continued their meaningful conversation and catch up. They chatted for a couple of hours before Maya took a taxi back to Brenda's place.

Tito Eddy said that he hadn't taken early retirement. Despite what the company told everyone, he'd actually resigned. He could have taken advantage of company benefits by retiring, but he needed to show that he stood by his principles. He didn't like how the new owner of the company had tried to interfere with the way he worked. The oligarch wanted to twist the news to get people to buy the paper, even though the company was already doing well. In particular, when Tito Eddy raised the paedophilia issue with him, the owner dismissed the subject. He didn't want *The Pinoy News* to cover drugs, corruption and gambling unless he checked the articles first. Tito Eddy decided it was time for him to go, as the company was heading in a direction he didn't agree with.

'Media is the most powerful tool in the world with which to spread information, but it is also the most evil,' he said. 'It can manipulate every area of an issue to twist the truth and spread propaganda. I have been in this business practically all my working life and it saddens me that our profession has become this way. But I don't feel I have failed. In fact, I will do my best to carry on spreading the truth until my last breath – and without anyone trying to manipulate me. Always remember, Maya, there is nothing more meaningful about life than being yourself.'

Maya knew Tito Eddy to be full of life, energy and enthusiasm. He was a workaholic, but he was also a knowledgeable and intelligent man – a role model of a leader. But now he looked tired and fed up, and he even swore when he spoke, which was previously unheard of. His wrinkles were more prominent and Maya realised he was coming up to his sixty-fifth birthday.

After a busy weekend moving to Gina's apartment, Maya was raring to go back to work at head office. She discovered she was being moved to a different department and would no longer be writing for the *PN Saturday Special* edition. She was furious but she'd had an inkling all along that this was going to happen and decided to ride with the tide.

Maya wrote her final article as usual, but on second thoughts she decided this could be the right moment to introduce her most important subject. She took a gamble and sent the amended piece to the chief editor, Jose Reyes' office, but he was out of town and the article was passed on to his deputy, who approved it.

Chapter Nineteen

The Pinoy News Saturday Special edition ran Maya's article on the front page.

An Island Unmasked
By: Maya Wara

I lived on this beautiful island for ten months. One thing stops me from calling it a perfect paradise island.

IT IS STREWN WITH PAEDOPHILES!

Yes, you heard it. And nobody is doing anything about it.

Let me tell you some of the things I saw and learned during my time on the island.

- I went swimming one day and met a nine-year-old girl who was clearly being abused by an old white man who acted as her stepfather.
- I befriended a local man who as a teenager was sexually abused by a supposedly retired foreign priest. The local man subsequently tried to commit suicide many times.
- Children regularly went in and out of the cottages belonging to foreigners.
- I heard a mother wailing because these despicable men were abusing her children.
- Mothers were unable to protect their children from paedophile partners or husbands.

These vile, disgusting, son of a bitch paedophiles prey on young children and sexually abuse them.

Now, I have a few questions:

To politicians – Does the future of your country's children matter to you?

To religious leaders – What is it that you actually preach? Save souls or save your skin?

To business owners – How much money would you pay to save at least one child?

To parents – How would you feel if your child was a victim of these dirty old bastards?

I can only surmise that these inhuman beings don't just exist in Puerto Galla, they are scattered around the country and world.

Now, my biggest question to the public is:

What can we do as people and as a country to protect our nation's children and their future?

When we visit places, especially tourist areas such as islands, we go in full of excitement and leave with joy in our hearts. But let us ask ourselves – do we really care what's going on around us? Do we notice untoward goings on but ignore them and think somebody else will fix them?

I really do hope that from now on the answer is NO.

We share the responsibility to protect our nation and our children's future. SPEAK UP!

My dear, avid readers, this is my farewell article. After this publication, I will no longer be part of *PN Saturday Special* edition. Before I go, I would like to thank you all for your continued support and patronage. With a heavy heart, I now bow and say GOODBYE to you all.

Needless to say, Maya was summoned to an emergency boardroom meeting with the grey-haired new owner and others in high management, including Jose Reyes and his deputy. The deputy was clearly in trouble, but Maya thought all the blame would be put on her any way. Before anyone had a chance to say a word, she walked towards the oligarch and, looking him straight in the eye, handed him her resignation letter before quickly exiting the room.

As soon as she emerged from the building, a crowd of photographers and news reporters greeted her. She thought they must be waiting for a celebrity but then she heard them shouting her name. She was totally taken aback and tried to make her way through the crowd before recognising a voice to her right. It was Gina and she was with Edward, the photographer. Maya walked towards them.

Gina nodded and put the microphone to Maya's face. 'Miss Wara, do you think you will lose your job because of your article today?'

'No, I will not lose my job. I *left* the job I loved for many years. I can only repeat what a good friend and a respectable man told me recently, "There is nothing more meaningful about life than being yourself." Thank you.'

Maya was trying to get away from the crowd by passing through Gina and Edward, when a commotion started.

'He's back!' Gina whispered to Maya, and motioned for Edward to move out of the way.

As if Maya was no longer there, the reporters and photographers flocked towards the new arrival. Maya stood to the side, shocked by what she was seeing. Standing nearby was Keith Smith, with a microphone in front of him. He spoke eloquently and with an air of authority. 'My name is Scott Gordon. I am an international photographer and reporter. I can vouch for everything that Miss Wara wrote. You will soon see the truth. It is coming your way. That is all I can say, thank you.'

Keith had no problem sidestepping the crowds as he headed straight to Maya and bundled her towards a waiting car with blacked-out windows.

Such was Maya's shock and delight that she couldn't speak. As the driver started the engine, Keith filled in the gaps.

'I arrived early this morning,' he explained. 'I couldn't get hold of you but luckily I was able to reach Gina, who told me where you were.'

Keith paused to give Maya a kiss and he wrapped his arms around her shoulder. 'Oh, I missed you and I'm glad you're OK. I was so worried when my sister gave me your message. I was due to come back today anyway, but I took an earlier flight.'

Maya started to sob, her emotions suddenly giving way. 'Thank you,' she mumbled as she buried her head in his now familiar chest. Then she remembered something. 'Scott Gordon?'

Keith laughed. 'Yes, that's my screen name as a photographer.' He tickled Maya and they both laughed. The driver took them to the Elite Hotel in Makati, and once safely inside their room, Keith briefed Maya about what had been going on.

That evening, Keith's intelligence team, together with the police, were going to Puerto Galla to raid the homes of the people on their surveillance list ... the ones who were also on Maya's. They had to do this simultaneously at dawn.

'It's taken time to get this far,' Keith said, 'but I'm glad all our hard work is coming to fruition.'

At the same time, other raids would be carried out in countries across the Far East. Maya also learned that while he was away, Keith had assigned a couple of IB agents to guard her on the island. Maya smiled over his thoughtfulness. With limited time together, Keith and Maya locked themselves inside their hotel room for a couple of hours. Then Keith dropped her off at Gina's before preparing for his team's midnight trip to the island.

The following day, news about the successful raid and crackdown on the Karnal paedophile ring across the Far East filled the world's media. This continued for several weeks and months as arrests, court trials and deportations went ahead one after the other. In total, 275 members were arrested – the majority of them in the Philippines and Thailand. The world was shocked, as it was revealed the perpetrators included famous singers and rock stars.

The main players of the successful raid, including international and national intelligence officers and the government agencies that had helped them, received great praise. But because of the nature of Keith's job, he couldn't be in the limelight. On the other hand, Maya, who was also credited with exposing the despicable crimes, had her name and photographs splashed all over the papers and she was deluged with interview requests. But she only agreed to give one, and that was with Gina. Her statement was short and to the point.

'I only did what anyone in their right mind would do under the circumstances,' she said. 'My work was only a tiny dot compared to the careful surveillance, diligence and utter brilliance of all the intelligence officers involved. Last but by no means least, I also want to thank the people of Puerto Galla for their cooperation, especially those who helped me with my research. May you continue to love and protect your beautiful island … '

Chapter Twenty

It didn't take long for Maya to land another job. She was hired by an international magazine called *The Asian Travel Digest* and was given her own column entitled 'Maya's Bird's Eye View'. She loved the name and agreed to it instantly.

As a child, she'd often wondered why her parents had given her such an unusual name. She finally asked her father after being teased by her playmates. They had been chanting her name while flapping their arms. She fondly recalled the moment when her father, Nicolas Wara, who was a most respected mayor in their town at the time, sat her on his knee while seated on his favourite armchair on their porch. He told Maya how since being a little boy he'd love birds, particularly the Maya. The country's tiny national bird was brown and white in colour. It was also common in most areas. But despite its diminutive size, it had a robust character. Its eyes looked tame and humble, but they also carried an air of knowledge and wisdom. It could spot its prey easily from afar, as well as any dangers.

Following the explanation, Maya's father had held Maya's chin and looked into her eyes. She would never forget his big smile as he told her how tiny she was when she was born. However, her eyes were big and tame looking, just like the Maya. He also explained that his great grandfather had chosen the surname Wara as it was the reverse of Araw, meaning 'day' or 'sun'. He added that he preferred sun because it symbolised warmth, brightness and mystery.

The Asian Travel Digest was published on a weekly basis, and sometimes Keith contributed his photographs and insightful commentaries as a tourist. The couple settled in Maya's apartment in Manila while continuing with their careers.

Maya enjoyed travelling the country for her column. She covered the main islands of Luzon, Visayas and Mindanao, as well as the smaller inhabited islands. The Philippines consisted of over 7000 islands, albeit not all inhabited, so it would have been impossible for her to cover them all. Sometimes, she was required to fly to other Asian countries to cover significant tourist destinations.

Maya's very first article in her new job was about Puerto Galla's enchanting waterfall. The headline read, 'The

Hidden Waterfall and The Mythical Lavinia'. It received good reviews and the islanders eventually started to open up about it. Before long, it had become a tourist hotspot.

On one occasion, Maya went to Pandacan Island, a small island commonly known in previous decades as 'Leper Island' because it was where people with leprosy were taken to recover in isolation. She discovered how beautiful it was and wrote about its underground rivers, lagoons, pristine beaches and thriving wildlife. To Maya, it was a true paradise and she featured it a number of times in her column.

Keith continued to switch between his photography and intelligence work. He accompanied Maya on her travels whenever he could and they enjoyed being together. He joined her on one of her visits to Pandacan Island and was blown away by the island's outstanding beauty.

As usual, Keith also travelled to other countries when required. At one point, he was sent to Colombia for six months to tackle the drug cartels. During this time, Maya was extremely worried and they both struggled with being away from each other for such a long period. When he finally returned, Maya went to fetch him from the airport. She waited in arrivals for nearly two hours before starting to worry. The flight had arrived an hour earlier but Keith was nowhere to be seen. She was about to enquire at the information desk when she heard her name being called. She turned around and saw Keith coming into the arrivals hall. He had a full-grown beard and looked strange. He was wearing what looked like an oversized white t-shirt with bold writing on it, which he'd tucked into tight jeans. As silly as he looked, Maya was elated to see him. She ran to him like a child and buried her face in his chest, hugging him tight. Keith slowly lifted her chin and briefly kissed her lips. He then took two steps back and spread his hands over the front of his shirt before taking something from his pocket. It was only then that Maya noticed what was written on Keith's shirt in capitals.

"MAYA, MY LOVE, WILL YOU MARRY ME?"

Maya's eyes were suddenly wet with tears. She'd never thought about marriage – not in a million years – she didn't think it was necessary without a child coming into the picture. But Keith had dropped to one knee and held before him a small, half-open box.

'Will you marry me, please, my sweetness?' he asked. His eyes were very serious and his voice betrayed a hint of nervousness.

Maya took the little box from Keith and helped him up. 'Of course I will, you silly thing. I do love you so.' She giggled and Keith suddenly lifted her up into the air.

'Oh my, sweetie, thank you. I was so nervous that you would say no. I love you, I love you, I love you.'

With that he swung her round and round.

The arrivals hall had emptied by then, but the few people around them stopped and clapped while giving their good wishes to the happy couple. Maya didn't hear much of it, as she was overwhelmed by what had just happened. They both composed themselves and Keith took from the little box that Maya was holding the most stunning heart-shaped, platinum diamond engagement ring. He carefully slipped it onto Maya's left hand ring finger. Maya had never seen anything so beautiful and they kissed as if no one else was in the room.

Keith put his arms around Maya as they walked out of the airport towards her car. A porter followed with his luggage.

Six months on, they were married in the only chapel in Puerto Galla. It was important for them to say their vows on their favourite island, where their love had blossomed. Maya looked stunning in a simple but elegant long, cream dress. Keith amazed everyone by wearing a kilt from his family's clan. Some of the guests thought he was wearing a skirt and he politely explained otherwise whenever he could.

They hired the Beachfront Hotel for the reception and partied until the early hours with their friends and acquaintances from the island, including Renato and his family, Aida, Berto, and many others. Maya's only family, Auntie Lina, Uncle Larry and her cousin Cora, who was then a student, flew and sailed out to be with them, as well as some new and former colleagues from Manila. Keith's sister Katriona attended with her husband Gerry and their two teenage boys, Harry and Connor.

'If only our parents were still alive,' Katronia commented. 'They would have loved to have been here.'

Sadly, Keith's daughter Penny couldn't get time off school to come to the wedding. Despite this one disappointment, the newlyweds had the most amazing time. All their guests enjoyed themselves and were impressed by the island's beauty. Most of them stayed on for a few more days and Katriona and her family loved it so much they extended their trip for another week. The boys were over the moon to get the chance to go scuba diving.

After Katriona and her family had departed for London, Keith and Maya travelled to the Scottish Highlands for two weeks for their honeymoon. They visited many tourist attractions, such as Iona Island and Eilean Donan Castle. They also went to see Keith's birthplace, the village of Alban. He reminisced about his childhood days and took Maya to see some of the places he knew.

Keith retired from his job as an ISAF agent when he turned 45 and put the wheels in motion to fulfil his dream of moving to Scotland. Maya sold the properties she'd inherited from her parents, keeping only the family home, which she intended to keep forever. A caretaker resided there and she only stayed when she visited her parents' graves.

After saying tearful goodbyes to all their friends and family, including Auntie Lina, Uncle Larry and Cora, who was crying uncontrollably, the couple left for Alban, living happily and quietly ever after ... until now.

PART THREE

Chapter Twenty One

While Maya waited for her transfer flight in Seoul, she phoned Keith, as they'd previously agreed, to update him on her journey. She also managed to speak to Auntie Lina, who was delighted that she was on her way. Cora needed all the support she could get. The last few days had been very long and emotional. The police had found the body of a young girl in a creek just outside Manila, but the family were still waiting to identify it. At the end of their short conversation, Auntie Lina informed Maya that her uncle would fetch her from the airport.

Maya was sitting in the departure lounge when two men and a woman settled themselves on the opposite chairs. They were talking in *Filipino* so Maya said hello and they exchanged a few words. They seemed surprised she could speak their language. The woman said they'd thought she was Indian and Maya smiled and said she'd take it as a compliment.

One of the men, Mark, was an engineer working in Saudi Arabia. Michael was a nurse based in Denmark and Julie was a nanny to a family in Canada. They'd got chatting while waiting for their connecting flight to Manila. They made Maya welcome in their conversation, which turned to politics, and she gladly joined in.

'I am very glad that President Roberto Amore won the elections last year,' Mark said. 'I am excited to go home and see for myself some of the changes that my family have been talking about.'

'Me too,' Julie said.

'I didn't vote for him, but I totally support him now,' added Michael.

'I hadn't really heard about him before,' Maya admitted. 'I went for the female candidate, Maria Salvador. When I was living in the Philippines, I knew of her as a tough, well-respected lawyer. I was sad when she passed away just a few months after the election. But as you do, Michael, I now support President Amore. Regardless of what the local and international media have to say against him, I think he's the real deal and truly wants to make the Philippines a better country.'

'Have you lived abroad for a long time?' Julie asked. 'I've been in Canada for nearly a decade.'

'Yes, I've been in the Highlands of Scotland for more than 20 years. For personal reasons, I was never very interested in politics, which is why I didn't vote even when

I lived there. But last year I decided to have my say as I'd always admired one of the vice-presidential candidates. Unfortunately, a miraculous wind seemed to sweep the results screen during the last hours of the count and he lost. That was truly unbelievable. I heard it described as like a thief in the night. I followed the results on the news and the internet, but I just couldn't believe what was happening in front of my eyes. To me, the vice president I voted for is the one who should have won.' Maya shrugged her shoulders with frustration.

'I couldn't believe what happened too,' said Julie. 'As far as I'm concerned, it was a total farce.'

'I must admit, I was mainly concerned about the results for my presidential candidate,' said Mark, 'but when I saw what was happening with the results I realised that the dirty politics we've been witnessing in our country for decades were at work again. Why in the world would you use a Killomatix electronic vote counter that had not been properly vetted and was known to have had serious problems for a significant national election? I am pretty sure the answer is the big word C!'

'Does that stand for big cunt?' Michael joked.

'A big cunt in corruption maybe!' Julie giggled.

'I prefer your offer, Julie,' Maya said, joining in the laughter. She had read previously about the Killomatix electronic vote counter, a computer program that was used to scan ballot papers and automatically upload and count the votes during the last general elections. The use of the machine was controversial, as it was open to manipulation, especially by the programmers themselves. As she read and heard more about the controversy surrounding the recent general election results, Maya was increasingly convinced that manipulation and corruption were indeed involved.

Julie broke their contemplative silence by saying, 'We could just laugh about our frustrations, but the good thing is that the current administration is delivering on its promises. And I am so happy that I can finally prepare to retire back home, as it's a much better place to live now.'

'Oh yes, no doubt about it,' Mark agreed.

The announcement came to prepare for boarding and they all stood up and wished each other a safe journey home.

On her flight from Seoul to Manila, Maya got chatting to a lady called Carmen Philips, who was seated next to her. She was a Filipina and was married to a British man called Alan. They'd lived together in London for over ten years.

'Whereabouts in London are you based?' Maya asked Carmen after they'd had their breakfast.

'In Clapham,' Carmen replied.

'Oh, that's not too far from Wimbledon, eh? We once went to watch the tennis championship and I think we had to change trains at Clapham Junction. I remember it well because we took the wrong connecting train and had to go back.'

Maya giggled as she recalled how she and Keith frantically

scrambled off the train when, after a few stops, a woman got on and asked with a very loud American accent if the train was heading to Wimbledon. Someone had shouted back that they needed to be on the opposite platform. Keith and Maya joined the American woman and finally boarded the right train. Their travelling companion had been very chatty and was excited to watch the Williams sisters, who were due to play against each other.

'That's right, it's not that far,' said Carmen. 'When some friends got tickets to Centre Court last year they came to stay with us. It's quite handy, as the train station is only a five-minute walk away. How about you? Where in Scotland do you live?'

'In the Highlands, a village called Alban,' Maya replied.

'Wow! I can just picture how relaxing it is to live there. I've never been but I've watched documentaries and read about them. I'm not sure about the infamous midges though!'

They both laughed.

'Yep, they're the downside, but wearing the right gear and insect repellent helps fight them off,' Maya commented.

'By the way, are you staying in Manila or going elsewhere?' Carmen enquired.

'To Manila ... ' Maya felt a sudden jolt back to reality as she remembered why she was going there. She quickly told Carmen about Nina, her cousin's missing daughter.

'Oh my God, bless her. I hope she will be found alive and well,' replied Carmen. 'I'm very sorry to hear that.'

They were both quiet for a few minutes before Carmen spoke once more. 'What has the world become, eh? As if we don't have our own problems to deal with. I'm also visiting my family in the province, but I've got to look into my brother-in-law's prison situation.'

'What do you mean?' Maya asked.

'Well, my brother-in-law, Brian, retired early from his job as a mechanic in London and went to live in Manila with his Filipina girlfriend … ' Carmen hesitated, but realised she felt comfortable talking to Maya and continued. 'He sold up in the UK, bought somewhere to live and opened a business in his girlfriend's town. But three years on, in January 2016, he was taken to the Pootan Detention Centre. His girlfriend had accused him of domestic abuse and she also reported him for overstaying his visa.'

Carmen explained that while she didn't condone abuse, she couldn't believe it of Brian because he'd always been such a gentle and kind person. Carmen had never really liked the Filipina girlfriend, who Brian had met online, and she and Alan had tried to discourage him from moving abroad to be with her. But Brian was obviously smitten by her youth and beauty – she was 24 while he was 52.

'What an awful situation,' Maya commented.

'This is what I'm raging about, and I even feel a bit ashamed. Apparently, since the previous government brought in a policy to encourage people to report overstaying foreigners in return for a reward, many greedy or scorned men and women have flocked to the immigration offices to report their other halves or business partners. Most of them concoct stories in order to deport these helpless foreigners and keep their money, property and businesses for themselves. The foreigners have very few rights.'

Carmen went on to explain how the Immigration Department had sole jurisdiction over the foreigners, which meant they acted as judge, jury and executioner. No checks were carried out by any other related government agencies, such as the Justice Department. Often, the foreigners were kept in detention as long as the Immigration Department could get away with holding them, prolonging their agony. Corrupt officials often took this chance to squeeze as much money out of their detainees as possible until they gave up the fight and acquiesced to the bribe or extortion money.

'That's terrible! I never realised what was going on,' said Maya. 'But then so much has been going on in our birthplace over the past two decades, it's been hard to keep up!'

Maya felt a pang of shame too. Where she lived now, prisoners, whether foreign or not, were treated fairly well and had many rights. More so, anyone accused of overstaying their visa was given government assistance and help to repatriate them as soon as possible.

'It's very hard to accept that our beloved country has gone downhill,' said Carmen. 'I blame this largely on bad governance and corruption, but there's no doubt that people's attitude needs to change too. For a start, they need to vote carefully and wisely – there should be none of this succumbing to widespread vote buying.

'By the way, while we're on the subject, what chance do you think our current government has to make a real change to our country? I for one think it has a very good one.'

'I'm for that too,' Maya said, concurring with Carmen's sentiments.

The two of them went on to chat about the more general stuff in their lives, dozing between conversations. It didn't feel as though four hours had passed when at last the pilot announced they would shortly be landing at Manila airport. Maya and Carmen wished each other well with the purposes of their visit and exchanged contact details before parting ways.

The summer heat greeted Maya as she walked through Manila Airport. She'd been wearing a fleece and jacket and had to carry them, along with her suitcase and hand luggage, when she checked out.

She was amazed by the airport's transformation and even questioned whether she'd landed in the right place. There were lifts and escalators and even a moving walkway. Although the trolley she was using to push her luggage was awkward to manoeuvre, she resisted asking one of the porters for help. She knew from previous experience that they would demand an extortionate amount of money before handing the trolley back.

During one of her previous travels to the Philippines, when Maya went to have her passport checked at the arrival's desk, the female staff member blatantly asked for a tip. She then placed the passport on her desk while pretending to work on her computer. Maya pretended she hadn't realised what had been asked of her and stood there for several minutes. Realising that Maya wouldn't budge and seeing the queue getting longer, the staff member finally, not to mention rudely, handed Maya's passport back.

What a difference this time round! Every staff member Maya encountered was cheerful and helpful. It transpired even the porters weren't 'charging' for their assistance.

Sweat was pouring down Maya's face by the time she met Larry and his driver. Initially, she did not recognise her dear uncle. He looked a lot older since the last time she'd visited three years earlier. His face was thin and he looked very drawn. Maya ran to him and hugged him tight for a few minutes, unable to contain her tears of joy and sadness. She then took his right hand and held it to her forehead to bless. She always maintained this tradition of showing respect to an older relative or close friend.

'I'm very glad you're home safe now, my child,' Uncle Larry said, hugging Maya back and tapping the back of her head. His voice was husky and he coughed several times on the hour's journey to Cora's house. Maya decided not to press him for details.

As soon as their car pulled up in the driveway, Auntie Lina rushed out to greet Maya, giving her a big hug. She ushered her inside. Cora was sitting in the living room staring blankly at the floor. When Maya said hello, she got up and clung to her, while crying like a child.

'It's OK, my love, I'm here now.'

Maya could barely stop herself from sobbing too.

They all settled together in the living room and shared a mid-afternoon snack. At first the atmosphere was strained and Maya attempted to lighten the mood a little. She commented how different the weather was. Back in Scotland, they constantly had the central heating on. Here in Manila, the air con was blasting out, yet they still needed electric fans.

It wasn't long before Cora returned to her usual self a bit.

'Thank you for coming, *Manang* MaiMai.'

Maya loved it when Cora called her by this name. It reminded her that Cora was not only a cousin, but her little sister too.

'I'm sorry I couldn't talk much on the phone,' Cora added. 'I was in shock and I still am.'

'It's OK, dear *ading*. I wanted to be here as soon as I could. We will sort this out.'

'You know, I cannot accept that the girl they found is my little Nina. She is still very alive in here … ' – Cora touched her chest and kept her hand there – '… I just know it's not her. They haven't even asked us to identify the body.'

'The police explained that they were still trying to make the body presentable,' Uncle Larry explained. 'They're hoping it will be ready for viewing and identification tomorrow morning.'

Later that evening, friends and neighbours turned up at Cora's house to pray and sit in vigil for Nina. They had done the same every night since her disappearance. In the living room, they lit candles by the statues of the Sacred Heart of

Jesus and the miraculous Virgin Mother Mary.

When all the visitors had gone, the mood in the house became very sombre. It only lightened when Dino came out from his room and put a Barbie doll in between the statues. 'Goodnight, Ninapot,' he said. 'Here is your baby, she misses you a lot, as I do. See you soon, OK.'

He went over to Cora, hugged her and said he wanted to go to sleep. Cora forced a smile and nodded at Maya before carrying her son to his bedroom, which he shared with Nina.

'Dino only knows that Nina is away temporarily and will be back home soon,' Auntie Lina explained.

With Cora out of the room, she felt she could finally tell Maya the details of recent events. 'After Cora dropped Dino at school on that dreadful morning, she walked with Nina towards the nearby day centre for Nina's morning class ... ' She paused and glanced at Uncle Larry, who nodded his head. 'Suddenly, a motorcycle stopped just beside the walkway. The passenger quickly snatched Nina, put her in between him and the driver, and drove off. Two other motorcycles followed them. Cora said it all happened so quickly. All the people on the motorcycles were wearing helmets so she couldn't tell whether they were men or women. When Cora started screaming, people gathered around and eventually some policemen in the middle of their motorcycle patrol tried to chase the group, which quickly dispersed through the alleys.'

Auntie Lina was trying hard to control her tears as she recalled recent events.

'You're doing fine, love,' Uncle Larry soothed, grabbing her left hand as she continued.

'I always encouraged Cora to come and live in our province ... it's too dangerous here in the city. But she insisted on staying here because she felt more independent, and her dental clinic is also doing well where it is ... '

After a short pause to catch her breath, Auntie Lina carried on. 'That evening, some police officers came here and asked Cora for details about Nina. They wanted to know her age, hair colour, what she was wearing, and so on. They then said they'd found the ... the body of a young girl by a small creek just outside Manila. They thought it could be ... it could be Nina.'

By this time, Auntie Lina was trembling and Uncle Larry held her hand even tighter.

The three of them chatted in the living room for a few minutes. Then Maya's two elderly relatives said goodnight before going to bed in the spare room. Maya was to sleep in Cora's room, while her cousin shared with Dino. She was knackered but managed to text Keith with an update before drifting off.

Chapter Twenty Two

The following morning, the police turned up to inquire who could come to the station to identify the girl's body. Cora said she would go, but only with Maya there for support.

Cora could not bring herself to look at the body, so Maya went in first. As soon as she lifted the cover she put it back down again. The face of the cadaver was disfigured, but she had seen all she needed to. She shook her head and headed back to where Cora was standing. In response, Cora rushed towards the body and lifted the cover herself. She paused, before lifting it some more until the whole body was exposed. Then she gently put it back and murmured a little prayer.

Before they left the police station, Cora and Maya were asked to sign some documents confirming the body wasn't Nina's.

'I'm really sorry about this, Mrs Bautista,' said the chief officer. 'I can assure you we will reopen the missing person's case and start searching for your daughter again immediately. We will also put out a public appeal. It would be a good idea for you to help by posting something on social media.'

'Thank you, sir. One of my friends put something up on the day Nina disappeared and I will too. Please, sir, do your best to find my daughter.'

The officer nodded. 'We will do our utmost, Mrs Bautista. And I will update you as soon as I have some news.'

∂

'I know my Nina is still alive, I can feel it,' Cora sobbed as she and Maya left the police station.

They took a taxi back to Cora's house and informed their family and friends of the news. Although they were initially relieved that the body wasn't Nina's, Cora's anxiety kicked in when they started talking about how they were going to find her.

Maya and Cora spent the afternoon posting pictures of Nina and the details of her disappearance on Facebook, Twitter and Instagram. They also contacted the local and national newspapers.

Maya was not really familiar with social media. Although she had a Facebook account, she seldom used it and had only logged on after the elections to read posts about the newly elected president. Nowadays, she only used it to contact her family and close friends. However, she shared Cora's posts and made them public viewing. Her former colleague Gina saw them and contacted Maya immediately. They met up that evening.

Over the past two decades, Gina had done well in both her personal and professional life. She was now Mrs Gina Morales-Santos and had a teenage son. She explained how she had left *The Pinoy News* two years after Maya. The company had become extremely partisan and she didn't agree with most of the stuff they wanted her to cover. Although the media outlet changed names a few times, the owner remained the same. Gina reckoned they changed the name to avoid paying tax.

Gina had moved on with her career and currently had a weekday morning radio talk show and an afternoon television one. Her husband, Eric Santos, produced them both. It was what she had always wanted to do and she was very happy with her life.

Gina updated Maya about some of their former colleagues and friends. Edward had left *The Pinoy News* at the same time as Gina to begin his own photography business. He also set up a training centre. When Maya asked about Tito Eddy, Gina lit up.

'Tito Eddy is the same Tito Eddy as he always was, Maya. He's as funny, witty and intelligent as ever. I took over his radio show when he hesitantly retired five years ago at 80, but he comes in as my occasional guest at least twice a month. People love him dearly and miss his show.

Unfortunately, he's been very unwell recently.' Gina's smile faded. 'It would be a good idea for you to visit him while you're here. I'm sure he'd love to see you.'

'Oh yes, I'll certainly do that,' Maya replied. 'Thanks for mentioning it. From now on, I shall use more of these modern technologies to communicate and get updates on friends.'

'Oh, and by the way, do you want to know about your ex, Arthur? I wasn't sure if you would.' As she spoke, Gina looked Maya directly in the eye.

'Oh, what about him?' Maya queried with a raised eyebrow. 'I'd forgotten he ever existed in my life.'

'Well, he was jailed for supplying illegal drugs to celebrities in the Makati bars. But somehow he was allowed out just before the national election campaigns began. He became one of the lead campaigners for the opposition to our current president.'

Maya was thoughtful for a moment. 'I am not surprised,' she eventually said. 'He definitely had a dark side. Now, whatever happened to the arrogant Chief Editor, Jose Reyes?'

Maya diverted the conversation, as she did not want to dwell on Arthur. The man no longer meant anything to her.

'Oh him,' Gina mused. 'He's still with the company. I call him the spin doctor of their fake news!'

The following morning, the news about restarting the search

for the missing girl made the front page of the papers. Gina interviewed Cora for both her radio and television shows. She was very nervous and emotional throughout, but she managed to put on a brave face. Over the following days, the stations repeated Cora's plea for help.

Maya tried her best to follow every lead they received and Cora accompanied her on some of them. At one point, they heard that an addict was holding a young girl hostage in one of the drug-infested areas of Quezon City, just outside Manila. Apparently, the girl had been held captive for hours and the addict had no intention of giving her up. Uncle Larry's driver took Maya and Cora to the house where she was being held.

As they approached the cordoned-off area, they could see that many curious and anxious people had already gathered there, along with some reporters and photographers. Cora asked if anyone had seen the girl, but no one had.

Meanwhile, Maya could see a woman trying to calmly mediate with the hostage taker. The man was behind a fence so Maya couldn't see him, but he was supposedly pressing a sharp dagger so close to the girl's throat that she could hardly breathe. This had been going on for eight hours in broad daylight and the deranged man was getting more and more agitated and nervous. It was clear that he may snap at any time, and that the girl was in imminent danger.

Plain-clothed policemen were dotted all around. One of them climbed up a ladder on a building behind the fence in order to get a good view of the hostage taker. Another joined him and together they positioned themselves and waited for a signal from the mediator.

Cora's heart stopped when gunshots and screaming suddenly filled the air. One of the policemen on the ladder had shot the hostage taker dead. People moved closer to the scene. The girl was screaming at the top of her voice. Blood poured from her throat as medics quickly escorted her to the waiting ambulance and rushed her off to the nearest hospital. Maya and Cora caught a glimpse of her and quickly established that she wasn't Nina. The kidnapped girl was at least 10.

The incident was covered live on the TV and radio and garnered so many differing reactions from the public. Was killing the hostage taker the right decision? It appeared there were only two choices; save the girl or let her die at the hands of the deranged addict.

Maya and Cora went back home feeling drained, tired and very upset.

The following morning, Maya went to the national library and read some newspapers from the archives. She was horrified by the sheer enormity of drug-related crimes. Almost every day, the front pages were filled with every type of crime, including kidnapping, murder, rape and torture. Most of them were allegedly related to the horrible *shabu* or methamphetamine. One tragic story that caught Maya's eye was of a grandmother who'd been raped, tortured and discarded in a layby by her own drug-addicted grandson. Another story brought shivers to Maya's bones. It was of a toddler who'd been raped, tortured and cut into pieces by her addict uncles.

Maya could not bear to read any further. Until the elections, she hadn't realised the extent of the drug problem in her country. The president had started a Fight Against Illegal Drugs (FAID) campaign. Even then, to see and witness it happening made the subject more poignant. She was at least glad that since the campaign began, millions of drug addicts had surrendered. That meant there were fewer zombie people in the streets committing these horrific crimes. By the time she left the library, Maya felt physically sick.

Instead of going back to Cora's house, Maya took a taxi to the local jail, where many drug addicts were detained. She wanted to see for herself the type of people who had ruined not only their own lives, but those of many others. She told the jail guards she was a novelist and wanted to see the conditions within a real jail for a book she was working on. The ploy worked and one of the guards accompanied her on a walkabout. He took her to a warehouse-like building split into sections by iron bars. Each section was cramped with men lying about almost on top of each other. A couple were reserved for the female prisoners. Most of the inmates looked dazed, confused and in dire physical condition. They definitely needed help. Maya had felt angry when she read about the appalling crimes these prisoners had committed, but now she felt enormous pity for them.

As Maya and the guard walked towards the exit, she asked what kind of help the detainees received. The guard explained how hard it was to manage the overcrowded jail and how they couldn't wait for construction on a rehabilitation centre to finish. The detainees would be moved and given the help they so desperately needed. Maya thanked the guard for his tour and took a taxi back to Cora's house.

That night, Maya went to her room right after the prayer vigil. Things were happening so quickly and it was making her depressed. She phoned Keith and talked to him for a couple of hours. As usual, he helped to soothe her shattered nerves.

Chapter Twenty Three

The following day, Maya went to visit Tito Eddy. Elena let Maya in and led her to his bedside. He lit up when he saw her.

'Oh, Maya, my girl!' he said, grabbing her hands. 'I knew you would come. How I missed you.'

He was lying in his bed with a drip in his right arm. He looked so frail, but his mind was as sharp as ever.

'I have so many things to talk to you about,' he said. 'This country has been lost and diverted for decades, but now it's awakening to a long overdue recovery.'

He took a deep breath and Maya remembered that if he talked in parabolic, there usually followed a significant and long lecture about life.

'I missed talking to you too, Tito Eddy, and I'm so happy to see you again. I wish I'd had the chance to hear you doing your radio talk show. I could have come and watched you in the studio.'

Maya tried to sound cheerful and didn't dare reveal what had brought her to her home country.

Tito Eddy grinned. 'Oh, yes, I miss my radio show. It kept me talking and I felt alive every time I did it. I'm very happy that our own lovely, bubbly Gina is doing it now. I'm sure she will do a superb job of keeping it going.'

As he spoke, Tito Eddy made a thumbs-up sign.

'Oh, I'm sure she will,' Maya agreed.

'By the way, have you been updated about what's going on in our country? Well, apart from what you may have seen or heard through the international media, of course.'

'I'm afraid I have been very naïve and disengaged from it all and I feel awful,' Maya admitted. She felt truly guilty and embarrassed for not knowing how much the country had changed in the decades she'd been away.

'Well, my dear, there hasn't been much to be delighted about, if that makes you feel better. I have watched the country go from bad to worse to even worst, to say the least! Politics, corruption and drugs were all interrelated. In short, for two decades, narco-politics has totally ruined the nation.'

Tito Eddy's strong words shocked Maya. He had always been so softly spoken, and in times of difficulty he often used diplomacy.

'You heard about the FAID campaign that the current administration implemented, right?'

Maya nodded.

'Over three million drug addicts have surrendered since this policy was implemented. These people were victims, too, of the narco-politicians, the drug protectors, the drug lords, the drug suppliers, the drug dealers and the drug itself. Putting to one side the usual drug-related offences that have always occurred in this country, most of the crimes committed in recent years were caused by methamphetamine or *shabu*. The root of the problem has to be stopped and this has to start from the top. And it's a very big task!

'The biggest problem is that some corrupt leaders and high officials from previous administrations are still embedded in the current one. And corruption exists to the core of the country's legal and justice system. It would be an enormous job to get rid of them all. I pray that people stay with the president in fighting these monsters of our nation.

'And by the way,' he continued. 'Do you remember the Rolanda funds that were raised by foreign countries to help the victims of the deadly typhoon we had?'

'Of course.'

'I believe the good-hearted, generous people from your side of the world were some of the biggest, if not the biggest, donors. The campaign raised millions in US dollars. Convert that to our currency and it would have been billions, which would have been more than enough to rebuild the lives of the poor victims. But sadly, my dear, only a fraction – if any – went to the real victims.'

Maya nodded, the expression on her face posing a question.

'Oh, don't ask me where it all went. I don't bloody know! There isn't a lot of concrete evidence to show that the previous government used it for the victims. Most of them are still picking up the pieces of Typhoon Rolanda's wrath.

'It was widely rumoured that crooked politicians used the funds for their campaigns during the last national elections. I am so embarrassed for my country, and so, so angry. No wonder it has been dubbed the 'sick man of Asia' for so many years. My dear, Maya, what has our beloved country become?'

Tito Eddy wiped away a tear and Maya offered him a cup of water to drink, which he gladly accepted. He took another deep breath and smiled this time. 'As I mentioned earlier, this nation's recovery has now started. I watched in despair as our country bellowed for help for decades. No one rose to the challenge until President Amore was catapulted into power. I can now die in peace knowing that the clean up of my beloved land has started, and may it last until the end. I owe a lot to our Mr Iron Fist!'

'You're not going to die yet, Tito Eddy,' Maya protested.

Her mentor shook his head and continued. 'Things happen for a very good reason. The rise of President Amore happened because it was meant to be. The international media make him out to be rude, crude, loud and disrespectful. I can only presume that he isn't favoured because he tells it as it is on the issue of colonialism. The President has been trying to demonstrate that colonised countries have different perspectives to those of the colonisers. You may turn a coin over, but there's no denying that this took place and that many countries can't forget. Nowadays, these previously colonised countries would defend their nation's sovereignty whatever it took. And for another country to tell them what to do goes against the grain. Amore is right to point out how the West persistently interferes in the affairs of countries it does not fully understand. I tell you, our dear President is one in a million – a great strategist and an intelligent leader. He does the job well. May God bless him always.'

Almost as an after thought, Tito Eddy asked how Maya and Keith had been doing. Maya told him how she loved where she was because it was so quiet and peaceful. She still contributed articles to *The Asian Travel Digest* on a monthly basis and had slightly changed her title to, 'Maya's Bird's Eye View – From Afar.' She and Keith travelled to different countries at least five times a year. They hoped to cover every country in the world before becoming physically incapable of getting on a plane. Maya giggled as she recounted their plan and Tito Eddy grinned back. Maya also told him that she had started writing novels.

Tito Eddy was very pleased for Maya and urged her to keep fulfilling her potential in life. Maya reminded him of what he'd once told her – 'There is nothing more meaningful about life than being yourself.'

'It's been my motto all these years,' Maya said.

Tito Eddy's face brightened. 'Exactly!' he said. 'And now my end is coming, I have no regrets in my life whatsoever, because I have always been me!'

He chuckled and held Maya's hands. 'You are a very special girl, Maya, I knew it from the start.' He then lifted her hands to his lips.

Maya realised he was very tired. She said goodbye and told him she would see him again before she flew back to Scotland.

A breakthrough with Nina's case came when they read a comment on one of Cora's Facebook posts.

'An elderly woman has a very young girl staying at her house, whom she claims is her granddaughter. The girl looks similar to the one in your photos. Maybe it's worth checking out. I'll message you the details of the place.'

Cora was excited by the development and Maya had to remind her not to expect too much and to prepare for the worse. They contacted the police and were told that someone had just been in touch and that a team of plain-clothed policemen were on their way to set up surveillance around the elderly woman's house. Cora asked if she and Maya could go there too, but she was told it would be better for them to stay put. They would be notified of any developments.

It was a tense and long day for everyone, especially Cora. She was nervous, unsettled and couldn't eat. The past few restless days and nights were catching up with her and she was very weepy. She sat by the window practically all day, staring blankly outside until people started arriving at the house for the nightly prayer vigil.

Afterwards, and just when everyone was about to leave, police cars turned up and Nina came running into the house, straight towards her shocked but delighted mother. The girl was screaming, giggling and crying all at the same time. Everyone went back inside and they prayed together, thanking the good Lord for the blessing of the day, and for answering their prayers.

Maya excitedly phoned Keith that night and told him the good news. She said she'd be staying for a few more days and wanted to visit her parents' grave.

The next day, the news spread about Nina's successful rescue. Cora and Nina were interviewed for Gina's radio and television talk shows. Cora invited all her friends and neighbours over for a thank you celebration and she provided a feast of food for lunch. The mood in Cora's house that day was joyful. Five-year-old Nina enjoyed being fussed over, but she didn't have a clue what had actually been going on. She said she was told to stay with a *lola* because her mother and brother had to go somewhere.

The gang who took Nina left her with one of the member's grandmothers. They'd actually meant to abduct a high-ranking policeman's daughter, but took Nina by mistake. They left her with the elderly woman as they tried to figure out what to do with her. Her grandson convinced her that Nina was his long-lost daughter, whom she'd never met, which is why she'd agreed to take her. The young couple who made the comment on Cora's Facebook page also reported it to the police. They'd seen Nina's photograph on Gina's television show.

Cora decided to heed her mother's plea to move to the province with her children. Over the next few days she did what was necessary to move her home and clinic. She would leave the city with Lina and Larry. Cora decided to go with them and make the trip to her parents' grave.

Chapter Twenty Four

The day before the move, Maya went to the Makati Mall to shop for presents. While waiting for her taxi back to Cora's, she received a phone call from Keith, which she eagerly accepted. 'Oh, hello, honey! I was going to phone you when I got to Cora's house. I had to do a little shopping to take to the province tomorrow. I'm just waiting for a taxi now. How are things there?'

'Yes, I knew you were going to call me soon, sweetie, but I noticed this morning that Jani and Jano are due their routine check-ups, so I've got to get to the vet's ASAP before it closes for the day. We'll probably be back in about three hours, so I'll phone you then, OK?'

'OK, hon, no worries! Oh, moochy moochy, I miss my wee doggies. I hope they'll be fine. I love you and I'll speak to you soon, honey bunch! Take care.'

'I love and miss you, my love. Speak soon. I need to go, so bye for now.'

As she continued to wait for a taxi, Maya replied to Cora's text asking where she was, as dinner would be ready soon.

When Maya awoke she was completely disorientated. She couldn't move her hands and she quickly realised they were tied with ropes. The room was very dark. As she moved, she banged her head on the wall. She assumed she must be dreaming and tried in vain to wake herself up. She vaguely remembered getting into a taxi to go back to Cora's house, but she never made it. She realised something must have happened in the car. She'd been given something that had made her go to sleep.

In the here and now, it was very dark and she couldn't see a thing. A man spoke and said they were imprisoned in a little hut. He was being held for ransom and it was most likely that Maya was too. Another voice piped up in the darkness and although the words were mostly incoherent, Maya made it out as 'ransom too'.

She figured it must be past midnight. The first man told Maya it would be better if she could try and get some sleep, as there was nothing they could do.

'How can I sleep?' Maya cried. 'What is happening? Where am I?'

She still couldn't believe what had just happened.

Someone from outside kicked the door and shouted, 'Shut up and go to sleep!'

Maya sobbed quietly and must have eventually cried herself to sleep, because the next time she opened her eyes it was daylight. She peered through the small holes from inside the hut. They were in the middle of nowhere and surrounded by trees. It was obvious they were outside Manila.

The tiny hut was about four feet by three-and-a-half feet and there were about three feet between the floor and the corrugated iron ceiling. The walls were made from a mixture of wood and bamboo rods, with two tiny windows opposite the door. Uneven wood covered the floor. To Maya, it was nothing more than a shack. The three hostages were squatting against three separate walls and there was nothing else inside.

Maya got to learn a little bit about the other two hostages. One of them was a drug dealer who had a young family and wanted to come clean. His former suppliers were holding him captive, as they had lost money and wanted it back.

The other captive was Chinese and he spoke in broken English. He was one of the recruits of a Chinese drug gang who lured poor, desperate and unsuspecting people from nearby countries such as China, Vietnam, Cambodia, Laos and Indonesia. The vicious gangsters promised them the lucrative opportunity of a working holiday on one of the Philippines' beautiful islands. Only when they arrived in the country they were rounded up in a derelict building and made to cook and pack methamphetamine for street distribution. They were forced to live like animals in a very cramped space and were not even provided with enough food to eat. The Chinese hostage tried to escape by swimming to the mainland, but a drug gang picked him up by boat. When they realised he was an escapee from a known Chinese gang, they demanded a ransom for his return.

The three hostages were given some water and a tiny piece of bread each for breakfast. That was all they had to eat until late afternoon when they were handed a plateful of chicken with rice. Although the food was tasteless, Maya was so hungry she forced herself to eat some of it.

Two captors guarded the hut at all times. At one point, Maya needed the toilet and one of them untied the rope on her hand and directed her behind some bushes at the back of the hut. He kept a very close eye on her as she relieved herself.

Maya speculated about running far away, but where? She didn't know the place and she would risk being shot at by these horrible, dangerous people. She tried to sit down for as long as possible, as at least this way she was able to get some air, but the bandit soon shouted that her time was up.

Worries about what was going to happen prevented Maya from sleeping. She thought about how frantic Cora and the rest of the family would be. How could she tell them where she was? And then there was Keith, of course. How could she let him know what was happening? And would she ever see him again? Maya couldn't stop sobbing. She was glad that the other two hostages were fast asleep; she could hear them snoring.

Maya pondered over how her home country had deteriorated in the 20 years she'd been away. Yes, she had visited regularly, but she hadn't realised what had been going on because she spent most of her time with her family and close friends. There were occasions when she'd noticed something was amiss, but she never paid much attention. Her visits were always nostalgic for her.

On one such occasion, Uncle Larry had picked her up at the airport and as they left a policeman ordered him to stop, claiming he was speeding or in the wrong lane. Uncle Larry handed over 2,000 pesos and the policeman quickly grabbed the money and waved him on. When Maya quizzed her uncle, he said there was no point in arguing with the policeman. He knew he wasn't violating any traffic rules but the cop wouldn't have let him go if he didn't get anything.

'This is normal nowadays, Maya,' Uncle Larry said, shrugging his shoulders in despair. 'It's their way of life and there's nothing much we can do but ride with it.'

'But we can report them to their superiors, can't we?' Maya asked.

There was a hint of sarcasm in Uncle Larry's laugh. 'Ah, rest assured your complaint will go down the drain. The top brass get the biggest share of their collection!'

A few years earlier, Maya had just arrived in Manila and was in a taxi when she heard a radio news programme about several young men and women, mostly students, who had collapsed and died during an open-air concert in the car park of a famous mall. At the same time, reports of people collapsing and dying came in from elsewhere in Manila and the surrounding areas. Maya commented to the driver how horrible the news was.

'Yes, ma'am, but it's becoming the norm here,' the driver replied. 'Anyone can get hold of *shabu* now, especially students. It's very sad, but you'll see, the story will be out of the news by tomorrow.'

'Really, why is that?' Maya enquired. 'Aren't the authorities going to catch those responsible?'

'They'll pretend to at first, then it will just die, just like it never happened at all,' the taxi driver said with a sigh.

Maya was perplexed. 'I feel so sorry for the families of the victims. They should put pressure on the authorities; the police force or the politicians.'

'Well, ma'am, as far as I know, they don't really care. My own humble opinion is that most of them are part of it!'

True enough, when Maya reached the province, the recent deaths in Manila weren't being reported on the news. Eventually, the story disappeared and the incidents most likely covered up.

Maya's recent conversation with Tito Eddy was beginning to make more sense. Corruption, politics and drugs were all interrelated and bad things were blatantly happening everywhere.

Chapter Twenty Five

Maya tossed and turned as she tried to get some sleep. She felt uncomfortable lying on the hard floor of the hut. She thought how at least it wasn't cold at night. Her mind was racing with so many questions. She wondered why someone would kidnap her. What did her captors want? Was it really the ransom money, like the other two hostages had implied? But how would they know she could afford to pay it? Or was this related to Nina's kidnapping?

Oh, how she longed for her ordeal to end. She also pondered some more over how long it would take for her country's ordeal to end.

Maya smiled in the dark as she held on to her hopes. She thought about the country's national election last year and how overwhelming the support for the current president had been. Filipino people had finally found hope. His tough stance against corruption, illegal drugs and poverty was strongly implemented as soon as he went into office, even amidst the furore the opposition created via the media.

Prior to the elections, Maya hadn't known much about this presidential candidate, and at first she wasn't sure about him, but her admiration grew as he started delivering his promises to the country.

By listening to his speeches, Maya learned more about the dreadful condition her country was in. She discovered how it was swamped with illegal drugs, especially methamphetamine, or *shabu* as it was locally called, and this had destroyed millions of lives. It was the first time that Maya had heard the term 'narco-politics', which referred to the way in which elected politicians were heavily involved in the proliferation of illegal drugs and were consequently the protectors of such crimes.

Every time Maya listened to the President's speeches, she felt his sincerity and love for his country. Yes, he used expletives, but who wouldn't if the one country you loved the most had been for years treated like a pigsty and abandoned to depravity? To Maya, the President was the epitome of a loving grandfather, a great protector and a natural educator. She had learned a lot from him since he came into power, including the tragic history of the southern part of the Philippines. When it was colonised by the West over a century ago, thousands of native southerners had been massacred. Throughout all her studies, Maya had never encountered this tragedy, as it was well hidden from most academic teachings. It was as if Filipinos had been educated the Western way, without being taught the atrocities the colonisers had committed. To Maya, it was clear that President Robert Amore was the real deal and he had her full support.

The new President was met with a great force of opposition from almost all directions as he implemented his tough policies. Many people didn't want the country to change for the better, as they wished to carry on fattening themselves while leaving the majority of Filipinos deprived of a better chance in life.

When these foul people realised the President wouldn't budge on his tough stance, they started to use the power of local and international media to spread rumours about his supposed dark side. By doing this, they even managed to influence some international organisations.

The media followed the president's every move, focusing on the way he cussed and picking over his smallest mistakes. They took every opportunity to malign him and to portray him as a negative and hateful person for the world to despise.

Maya knew all too well how the media played tricks. She felt she had a responsibility to defend her birth country's new leader in any way she could. Although not a fan of social media, she'd used Facebook to post positive comments about her country and its new leader. She found out that millions of fellow Filipinos around the world also went online to do the same, and Maya found this inspiring.

At one point, she became so emotional reading the comments posted by the new leader's many supporters that she found herself typing a prayer for her country. That was the first time in many years that she had openly prayed or written one. She shared it with her friends and also posted it on other bloggers' Facebook accounts.

Dear God,

Thank you for giving us the Philippines
As our beloved country.
Thank you for giving us a chance
To redeem the glory days
That you have intended for her.
Thank you for awakening us
With the truth,
And thank you for giving us a new president
To lead our country into
A new and hopeful beginning.

We believe that You are the only one
Who knows and understands exactly
The extent to which our country and her people
Have suffered over the years.
We believe that You are the only one
Who can restore her back
To the glory of her days.
We believe that You have listened
To the cries of the people.

We believe that You make things possible

In your most miraculous and mysterious ways
And in the most significant of times.

Our country is currently facing a huge battle –
A battle to free her
From the terrors of life –
Drugs, corruption and crime.
So that we can live freely
With the basics of life
That You have blessed us with.

There have been many lives lost
In this battle already.
If it is a sin to allow this to happen
For the benefit of the masses
We ask for Your mercy and forgiveness.
We also ask for the forgiveness of the sins
Of all those who have perished in this battle.
May their souls seek refuge
In Your loving arms
For You are a forgiving God.

We pray that You bless and take care of
Our dear President
In all aspects of his life, especially health wise.
Please help guide and protect him always,
Continue to give him the courage, strength and wisdom
To lead the country into a new and brighter society.

We pray for the people who help the President
In his quest to restore law and order for the country.
Please bless and help them to fulfil their duties
With love, honour and integrity.

We pray for all the perpetrators
Of these terrors of life,
May they be enlightened from the darkness
Of their wicked works and ways
And find Your presence in their lives once again.

For the innocent victims of this battle,
We pray that You hold their hands tight.
Embrace them with Your loving arms
As they follow Your path for them in heaven,
Where nothing else exists but peace and love.
May their loved ones here on earth
Find comfort with this knowledge
And find courage and hope to live
With love and forgiveness in their hearts.

Finally, may our beloved country and her people
Rise above all these terrors of life
So there is peace, forgiveness, love and harmony
And all of us unite.

We pray in Your loving son, Jesus Christ's name,
His words and His ways.
AMEN

There was a time when the newspapers in the UK carried negative stories about the Philippines and its new leader almost daily. Maya felt really hurt when she read the allegations that the leader was a mass murderer because of his FAID campaign. This was because the intense crackdown on drugs had led to the deaths of many drug pushers, drug lords and addicts. Many of them had been given the chance to surrender but had chosen to fight back and protect their illegal trades.

Maya wrote to and emailed all the main newspapers in the UK to give a positive outlook and another perspective on the story, but she received no replies. By this point, her frustrations concerning the international media were reaching boiling point and she decided to stop reading or watching the news.

Maya also wrote to international organisations in Europe that dealt with human rights and international crime, as well as the European Coalition, who were trying to portray the President as a killer and murderer. These foreign organisations, under the influence of those who opposed the President's administration, seemed hell bent on stopping him carrying out his fight against drugs. Maya wrote to them about the many positive results of the new President's efforts to make the country a better and safer place for the people, and how he was widely supported by many Filipinos living inside as well as outside the country. All she received were a couple of acknowledgements to her letters.

Again, Maya realised what Tito Eddy was referring to

when he said the West interfered with countries it did not fully understand.

Chapter Twenty Six

It was past midnight by the time Maya felt sleepy. She was just drifting off when she heard the door creak and some hoarse grunting noises. It was pitch black and she couldn't make out what was going on. Feeling nervous, she tried to sit up only to feel a hand suddenly touch her feet and attempt to pull her back down again. She let out a scream. The other two hostages woke up and asked what had happened. Someone from outside kicked the door wide open and flashed his torch around the tiny room. The man crouching next to Maya was naked. She realised he was the bandit guard who had previously escorted her to the toilet. He was clearly high on drugs. The other man pulled him outside and started kicking him.

'I told you not to touch the woman! We only want the

money. Remember what The Big Man said? He will kill us if we don't do what he says.'

Darkness enveloped the room again as the man closed the door. Maya was trembling with fear and she started to cry. The other two hostages tried to console her and told her to get some sleep, and that nobody would touch her again.

In between sobs, Maya pondered her faith. She'd lost her religious dedication when her parents died, but she considered herself faithful to God and believed she had her own personal relationship with the Creator. She seldom went to church except for special occasions, such as Christmas, Easter, weddings, christenings and funerals, just to show respect regarding where her faith in God had begun. But now she began to question even that.

'What have I done to deserve this?' she said out loud. 'Are you there, God? Please help me!'

One of the hostages made a noise indicating his impatience and murmured how he wanted to get some sleep.

Maya eventually dozed off and was woken by the loud thuds of someone pacing back and forth outside the hut.

'Have they had some breakfast yet?' someone with a very hoarse voice asked.

'Not yet,' replied the bandit who had dragged the would-be rapist out of the hut earlier. 'We're still waiting for the bread from Kaloy.'

'Give the woman her shopping bags and handbag,' the newly arrived bandit told the two guards. 'But give her mobile phone to me. Then untie her hands and bring her out here.'

'Yes, boss,' the two bandits replied in unison. They took Maya's things inside the hut and placed them in front of her before setting her loose. She quickly rummaged through her bags and was relieved to find that everything was still there, even her groceries. She was famished and opened a packet of biscuits, taking a few for herself before passing them onto the other hostages.

'Woman, you need to come out, someone needs to speak to you,' one of the bandits said.

Having not slept for the last few nights, Maya was more than a little unsteady as she pulled herself to her feet and followed the two bandits outside. A gangly man with a moustache was seated nearby. He was wearing sunglasses, a pair of blue jeans, a white polo shirt and a pair of black trainers. 'I believe your husband is in Scotland?' he said, before continuing without waiting for Maya to reply. 'I think you will have guessed by now why you are being kept here.'

Maya shook her head. 'No, I don't bloody know. Why the hell am I here? Tell me!'

'Hey, calm down, woman! The answer is obvious, of course, we want money from your husband.'

Just then, Maya heard gunshots. She was about to retreat inside the hut when the man grabbed her hand. The gunshots carried on one at a time for a few minutes before ringing out continuously, as if coming from a machine gun.

'Don't panic, the boys are only training,' said the man in the polo shirt. He then brought out Maya's phone and handed it to her. 'Phone your husband now!' he ordered.

Maya was trembling as she met the man's fiery gaze. She took the phone and started searching for Keith's number in her contacts list. She dialled and realised it must be the very early hours in Scotland. It was likely that Keith was asleep. The phone kept ringing and ringing until eventually a groggy sounding Keith picked up.

'Hon, listen. I'm being held hostage and they want some money … ' Maya began.

Keith knew Maya had gone missing and had been advised to wait for a call from her before travelling to the Philippines. Cora had texted him the night Maya didn't return home and he immediately contacted his former colleagues in Manila. One of them, Paul Panalo, was the new Chief Superintendent of the Intelligence Bureau (IB). He was the one who had advised Keith to wait for information, as the likelihood was that whoever had taken her would want a ransom. The chief reassured Keith that they would do their best to find her.

As soon as he realised it was Maya on the phone, he jumped out of bed.

'Sweetie, babe, are you OK? Where are you, honey?'

'Hon, I'm OK, but I don't know … ' Maya was cut off as the bandit man in the polo shirt grabbed the phone off her.

'Listen, mister. Give us ten million pesos within the next five days or you'll never see your wife again. Contact us on this number when you're ready and we'll tell you what to do with the money.'

The phone went dead. By this time, Maya was shaking. The amount they were asking for was about one hundred and fifty thousand in sterling. How was Keith going to get his hands on that amount of money at such short notice?

Chapter Twenty Seven

Meanwhile, in the busy tourist town of Carvate, a two-hour drive from Manila, an agitated man walked into a photography shop and bought dozens of batteries of various sizes and a few disposable cameras. The man behind the counter couldn't help looking at him. He was wearing sunglasses when he walked into the shop, but he took them off when he made the payment from his bulgy wallet. Then he rushed back out towards a waiting, blacked-out white van.

The man behind the counter was Edward Balera. He'd recognised the man – it was Arthur Manabo, his infamous former colleague. Arthur obviously hadn't recognised him. He wondered what he was up to this time.

Edward normally ran his shop in the mornings and taught his photography students in the afternoons. That afternoon, he took five trainees for a practical outdoor photoshoot in a woodland area he hadn't visited before. They were in the middle of their lesson when they heard gunshots. At first, Edward thought it was just someone cleaning their guns, but he thought otherwise when the sound didn't cease.

One of Edward's trainees, who lived locally, told of a rumour he'd heard about a gang of bandits who'd made a training ground in the area. Apparently, they also had huts, where they kept their hostages. He explained that the local people wouldn't report it, in case the gangsters came after their families. Edward became concerned for their safety. He tried to work out which direction the gunshots were coming from, so they could avoid them, but he decided he couldn't risk his group being hit by stray bullets. They packed up their equipment and headed back to the training centre beside his shop.

That night, Edward phoned Gina. After exchanging pleasantries, he told her about his unusual day. 'You'll never guess who came into my shop,' he said.

'Mmmm, you sound excited. I don't want to guess – I want to know, so tell me!' Gina said with amusement.

'Nothing exciting, really ... it was only our deceitful former colleague, Arthur. And he didn't recognise me!'

'Oh dear, what is he up to in your area, I wonder? I bet it's something fishy.'

Gina began to think seriously now. Arthur's name always brought a shiver to her bones. She'd heard on the grapevine how notorious he had become since he was jailed and subsequently pardoned by the previous government.

Apparently, after the defeat of the presidential candidate he was paid to campaign for, he was now a leader of a kidnapping gang.

'That's what I thought, too,' Edward replied. 'And I also learned today of a rumour concerning part of the forest around here. Apparently, bandits are using it as a training ground.'

'Really?! That's very interesting!' Gina exclaimed. She grabbed a notepad from her table and quickly jotted some stuff down.

Edward could tell by her voice that she would use her resources to look into the rumours.

'I'll leave that information in your most capable hands, shall I?' he teased.

'I shouldn't say it but yes, it's noted. And by the way, I'm glad you phoned because I was going to call you regarding Maya.'

'What about her? I read about the kidnapping of her cousin's daughter. I heard that she'd been successfully rescued. Does it concern that?'

'Oh no. That ordeal is over, but Maya herself is currently being held hostage by some bandits who are possibly looking for a ransom.'

Edward's mouth fell open. He was so shocked that he couldn't speak for a few seconds. 'Oh, no! That's so awful, especially after what just happened to her relatives. I really hope she is fine wherever she is, Gin. And how is Keith, have you heard from him?'

I spoke to him yesterday on Skype. He's very worried, as

you can imagine, but he said he will do whatever it takes to get Maya back. He's going to fly over as soon as he gets more information, as he was advised by his contacts here in Manila. He's keeping me in the loop too but asked for this not to go public. The authorities here are already working in the background.'

'That's good, but do let me know if there's anything I can do to help our friends,' Edward offered.

On the other side of the world, Keith couldn't get back to sleep. But he was at least relieved to have heard his wife's voice. He'd been extremely worried about her and even wondered whether any of this would have happened if he'd gone with her to Manila. He got up to make coffee. 'My Maya will hold on, I'm sure of it!' he said out loud as he paced back and forth across the kitchen. 'She is a strong and clever woman and she will get through this. We will get through this.'

Keith was prepared to pay whatever amount it took to get Maya, the love of his life, back safely. He had already arranged with his bank to take out as much as required and have it wired over to Manila so he could withdraw it. He contacted Cora, Gina and Chief Superintendent Paul Panalo to tell them about the phone call. They were all elated to know that Maya was alive. The Chief advised Keith to keep calm and told him to get to Manila as soon as he could.

After making a few more phone calls, including one to his sister Katriona to update her, Keith travelled to Glasgow and boarded the first available morning flight to Manila.

He arrived at 8am the following day, local time. Chief Superintendent Panalo and another former local colleague picked him up. They went to a nearby hotel to figure out their next move.

Keith phoned Maya's number that afternoon and a husky voiced man answered. He said that Keith should wait for a phone call back.

At 6:30 the following morning, the Booleebee restaurant next to the pier in Carvate town had just opened. One of the staff members was mopping the floor and another was wiping the tables and chairs.

After a few minutes, a loved-up couple parked their motorbike at the front and walked inside. They ordered their breakfast and some coffee and went to sit in the right-hand corner by the window.

A few minutes later, Keith walked in with a rucksack. He went to order a cappuccino and the woman behind the counter winked at him as she processed his payment. She motioned to Keith to sit in the left-hand corner by the window. Keith forced a smile and went to sit down with his drink. He was very nervous but excited at the same time. Soon he would be reunited with his dear wife. He checked his wristwatch and saw that it was 6:42am. The couple across from him were busy eating and sweet-talking with each other. They never even looked at Keith. At 6:45am, he went outside, leaving his rucksack on the table.

Chapter Twenty Eight

Maya was harshly woken at 5am by one of the bandit gang guards. She was told to gather her stuff together. The other two hostages were still fast asleep. Maya was a little puzzled, but she had an inkling that Keith was going to pay the ransom and that they were going to take her to the meeting point where the exchange would take place. But what if the bandits were just moving her to another hostage location?

Her hands still tied with rope, she was put in the back of a blacked-out white van. All her things were thrown in next to her. She couldn't see the driver or the passenger beside him. One of the bandits climbed into the back of the van and sat opposite Maya before the vehicle drove away.

At 6:50am, at the Booleebee restaurant, Maya walked in with a bulky short man who had his arms wrapped around her waist in an intimate way. Maya tried hard to keep calm. One wrong move and the gun pressed to her waist might go off. The pair walked towards the counter and ordered hot drinks. Maya's eyes widened when the girl at the counter smiled at her; it was Gina!

As the man looked about the room, Maya stared at her friend, who quickly winked and pointed her nose towards the table with the rucksack on it.

'You may have a seat, sir and madam,' she said. 'I'll bring your order over to your table.'

The couple seated at the right-hand corner continued to chat and didn't seem to notice Maya and the bulky man as they walked towards the table. The man's arms were still tight around Maya's waist. As they sat down, the man motioned for Maya to open the rucksack and show him the contents. Then she was told to close it again. He let go of Maya and grabbed the bag. As soon as he got up, Gina was at their table with the hot drinks. She threw the contents at the man, startling him. At this point, the loved-up couple seated opposite quickly stood up; the woman helped Maya get up while the man tackled Maya's captor before he shot the gun. The rest of the staff came out to help while Gina and the woman quickly bundled Maya outside towards a waiting, unmarked police van. Gunshots could be heard outside the restaurant as the bandits fought it out with the police and IB agents.

The woman took a seat at the front of the police van beside the driver while Maya and Gina climbed into the back, where Keith was waiting. As soon as they got in,

Keith grabbed Maya and kissed and hugged her tight. They couldn't untangle themselves from each other and nor could they speak. They were both so relieved and cried like children. Gina watched them with tears in her own eyes.

Once they had composed themselves, Maya and Keith embraced Gina and thanked her over and over again. Gina mentioned that it was Edward who had given her the tip off regarding the gangsters' location. She wasn't sure about it at first, but her gut feeling told her to pursue it with her own team and resources. The trio were driven back to Manila where they met with Chief Superintendent Panalo and other officers at a hotel. Maya gave statements about her ordeal.

It turned out that all the customers at the Booleebee restaurant before Maya and her captor arrived were IB agents. Well, all except Gina, who had volunteered to help her friend. The seven bandits who'd been in and around the restaurant area were captured; two of them were injured during the battle. One of the IB agents was shot in the arm, but thankfully his injury wasn't life threatening. It was a miracle that no one had been killed. The hut had been raided at the same time as Maya's rescue mission and all the bandits who were hanging about in the woodland area were captured too.

News of the rescue mission broke on Gina's radio and TV talk shows.

'Members of one of the most notorious gangs in the country were captured during an early morning raid,' said the newsreader. 'As a result, their two hostages – one a former drug dealer and the other a Chinese man who was recruited by gangsters to work in their illegal *shabu* factory on a remote Philippine island – managed to escape.'

Maya had asked the officers not to divulge her identity as a hostage. She wanted to downplay the incident and didn't want to be in the public's eye and under scrutiny once again. Consequently, nothing was mentioned about her own kidnap and rescue.

PART FOUR

Chapter Twenty Nine

The day following Maya's rescue was spent with the police and IB departments. A criminal case was to be filed against the abductors, but the authorities were still on the hunt for The Big Man, whom the bandits pointed to as the mastermind of all their illegal activities. The ransom money was returned to Keith and he deposited it back into the bank. Maya's mobile phone was held by the authorities to be used as evidence against the hostage takers, so she had to buy a new one.

It was early evening by the time Maya and Keith finished dealing with all the necessary paperwork for the criminal case. They were both famished and had a quick snack at a nearby fast food restaurant before being driven to their accommodation at a Makati suite hotel.

Once they got inside their spacious room, Maya went to

take a shower, as she had not washed for several days. Keith couldn't contain himself and after a few minutes joined his wife, gently putting his big arms around her naked body and gingerly rubbing soap all over her soft skin. He kissed her passionately under the refreshing rain of the warm shower. Maya felt the dirt, trauma and the nightmarish events of the last few days wash away as the water flowed smoothly over her skin and she felt Keith's blistering heat as he entered her.

Afterwards, they did not dare leave their hotel room and ordered room service. Maya phoned Cora using Keith's mobile and updated her on recent events.

'I'm so happy to hear that you're safe and with Keith now, my dear *Manang*. Mum and Dad were so thankful when we found out you were safe. Mum says that God is good all the time. She bursts out praying whenever she feels the need.'

Maya could hear the joyful relief in Cora's voice as she spoke. She knew and understood Cora's feelings, as just as one struggle had ended with her daughter, another had begun with her beloved cousin. It was just as well Cora had a strong character and was able to cope with all the trials of life that were thrown in her direction.

'I couldn't agree more with Auntie Lina,' Maya replied. 'Someone up there was definitely by the side of Nina and me. Listen, Keith and I have decided to stay here in the city for a few more days. If you want, you can go ahead with your move to the province and we'll follow in a few days' time. Please take my stuff with you and I'll get it when we go to visit Mama and Papa's house.'

'Sure. We're all set anyway so we will go ahead at midday tomorrow,' Cora replied. 'Say hello to Keith for us and see you both soon.'

During the first two days of their reunion, Maya and Keith stayed in their room all day and night; they slept, woke, ate and made love as if nothing else mattered.

At one point, as they lay in bed rested after another passionate session, Maya spoke in detail about her ordeal while Keith listened intently. As Maya got to the part where the addict bandit guard was going to rape her, Keith clenched his teeth. 'Bastards! They're lucky I didn't see them or I would've killed them all.' He was furious and held Maya tight to his chest. 'This will never happen to you again, my love, I promise. I love you so much.'

'I love you so much, too, my honey. I can't bear not to be with you.'

On their third day, after lunch, they decided to laze about by the hotel's rooftop pool. As they lay on the sun deck, Keith's phone beeped with a message from Chief Superintendent Paul Panalo. He said he wanted to see both of them at the hotel at 6pm, and that it was very important. They could talk over dinner in the hotel restaurant. After concurring with Maya, Keith agreed to the suggestion.

By the time they arrived, the Chief was already in the lobby waiting for them. He was not in uniform this time, but the way he stood and his aura gave off an air of authority. He was wearing jeans, a stripy navy shirt and a pair of black leather shoes. Maya didn't recognise him at first, but luckily

Keith did. After some pleasantries, the three proceeded to the restaurant.

'Thanks for meeting up with me at such short notice,' Chief Panalo said as they were ushered to their seats. Although the restaurant was fairly quiet, they were given a very private area.

'Oh, no problem at all, Paul,' Keith replied. 'We didn't have any plans for tonight anyway.'

'That's great. Oh, it's been a very busy day. I would've contacted you and met with you earlier, but I was called to an emergency visit at the Pootan Detention Centre.'

Maya's ears pricked up upon hearing a familiar name. 'Oh, that's a very interesting place,' she said and looked at Keith. 'Remember the girl I mentioned to you, whom I sat next to during my flight from Seoul to Manila? Her name is Carmen Philips and her brother-in-law has been detained at the Pootan Detention Centre since 2016.'

Keith eventually remembered; it was a topic that had come up during one of their many long telephone conversations since Maya had arrived in Manila. 'It's quite a sad story,' he said.

'I guess he's one of the foreign detainees at the centre then?' Chief Panalo asked.

'Yes,' Maya replied at once. 'Do you work there too?' Maya's curiosity was awakened.

'Not at the centre itself, but as part of the Intelligence Bureau support assigned there. I've been there hundreds of times, even when I was still an IB agent. I kind of know their words and ways.'

Maya noticed that Chief Panalo seemed a little embarrassed. 'What's the brother-in-law's crime then?' he asked.

Just then, the waiter came to put their drinks on the table. Maya waited for him to leave before she replied. 'Well, his name is Brian Philips and to cut a long story short, he was reported by his ex-girlfriend for domestic abuse and overstaying his visa.'

'Oh, that's a typical scenario ... and the ex girlfriend gets to keep all the foreigners' properties and belongings.'

Maya nodded. 'Looks like it.'

'You know, I've not been in this post for long, but I've already received numerous complaints from families and friends of past and present detainees. They claim that they are or were being blackmailed to pay extortionate amounts of money for the release of their loved ones. The problem is, it is out of our jurisdiction. We only entertain complaints and investigate them to pass on to the Immigration Department. They have all the power. But I do know the detainees may have valid grounds to complain ... ' He frowned before continuing. 'The problem is, institutional corruption seems to be embedded in a few greedy higher officers. However, due to the number of complaints we've had recently, which doesn't really surprise me, I've instructed our legal team to draft a resolution about our concerns and recommendations to the President. Hopefully, they can be acted upon as soon as possible ... it's actually the reason why I was there today, to finalise the draft.'

'Wow, that's really good,' said Maya, visibly lighting up. 'Change is coming then?'

Chief Panalo nodded but remained pensive for a few seconds. Then he took his notebook and pen from his shirt pocket and asked, 'What was your friend's name again, and his crime?' He then scribbled down the information as Maya provided it.

Their food arrived and the three of them happily tucked in, sharing personal information about the events in their lives as they ate. Years ago, when Keith was an ISAF agent, Chief Panalo was his main local IB partner. He was only a few years younger than Keith and was very passionate about his career, which meant he hadn't started his family until his late 30s. He was just married when Keith first met him and they used to joke about their loved-up and love-less lives. That was before Keith met Maya.

Chief Panalo was jovial as he relayed his family life. 'Before you ask, I have no intention of retiring just yet,' he laughed. 'I've always loved my job, even though it does add to my wrinkles sometimes. Besides, my two sons are all grown up now and have their own lives. My eldest is in the National Army and my second is studying to become a scientist. He wants to become an astronaut! To be honest, I don't know where he got that idea and interest from, probably the comic books he used to read when he was young. Anyway, I wouldn't know what to do with myself if I retired.' He paused and grinned at Keith. 'Mind you, I don't mind being with my darling wife, Rebecca. She's my

183

all time flower, every moment of the day, but it's just not the right time yet. So, how are you two in your lovely highland manse?'

'Well, life has been a good but boring one!' Keith joked. 'Our place is quiet but very comfortable. We travel at least five times a year and we learn new things in the process. Maya still does her part-time freelance writing in between our travels and every now and then I help her with some of the photography.' Keith looked at Maya, who was smiling and nodding her head in agreement. 'I also enjoy my favourite sport, angling, which thankfully I was able to learn and develop after I retired.' Keith's eyes glowed at the mention of his pastime. 'And, well ... I just had a thought ... something you reminded me about. I still have my journal containing all our 'exciting' adventures during my agent days, which is just waiting to be made into a story. Be prepared because a lot of the readers will become most familiar with you!'

'I can't wait. I will be privileged to be part of it,' Chief Panalo replied.

'Aha, I can't wait to read the secrets of the secret agents!' Maya said, joining in the laughter.

When they had finished their meal and eaten dessert, they ordered some drinks. Maya asked for a hot chocolate while Keith and Chief Panalo ordered a pint of beer each. Their order arrived quickly and the Chief straightened up in his chair, his mood changing from jolly to more serious.

'As I mentioned in my text message earlier, it was important for me to see you tonight. There have been some big breaks in our investigations over the last few days regarding the events you were involved in, Maya. First, the five-member motorbike gang who abducted Nina were all caught. Three of them confessed that they were ordered to abduct the daughter of a high-ranking policeman who was instrumental in the capture and imprisonment of a narco-politician connected to a well-known oligarch. We are in the process of verifying their claims and an investigation into the oligarch in question has already begun.'

Maya nodded and muttered, 'That's good news.' She couldn't resist adding, 'How about the girl who was found in the creek and mistaken for Nina? Have the killers been found yet?'

The Chief hesitated. 'Well, yes, the killer was arrested yesterday. Sadly, it was her own father, a *shabu* addict. He confessed to his wife and she called the police.'

'Oh my, that's a very sad case indeed, poor girl.' Maya was mortified and wished she hadn't asked the question. She felt repulsed by the Chief's answer.

Keith shook his head. 'No wonder the President has the full support of the majority in his campaign against illegal drugs. I totally agree with it.'

Chief Panalo brought out a couple of small photographs from his pocket and showed the first one to Maya. 'Do you recognise this person?' he asked.

Maya had to lean in to scrutinise the passport-sized picture of an older looking man, who was probably in his late forties to early fifties. 'No, I don't,' she replied.

Chief Panalo showed her the other photo and Maya's

185

eyes widened as she stared at a younger man's image. She looked at Chief Panalo. 'I recognise this one. That's Arthur Manabo, a man I used to be with ... '

Keith looked at the photo too.

'Well, those two photos are of only one man, and he is indeed Arthur Manabo. He is also The Big Man of the bandit gang who kidnapped you. He was the mastermind behind the operation.'

Maya's face went blank and she began to tremble. 'No ... it can't be?'

Chief Panalo nodded his head.

'I can't believe he's capable of such horrific actions, but then again I don't know the man anymore. I feel ashamed that he was part of my old life.'

'The bastard!' Keith muttered angrily.

'He was arrested this morning,' Chief Panalo explained. 'Which is one of the reasons I wanted to see you both, to personally inform you about what we've discovered and to let you know what needs to be done with the cases while you're still in the country. Of course, Manabo denies every allegation against him, but all the bandits pointed to him as The Big Man and the mastermind behind many kidnappings for ransom over the last couple of years. Apparently, he became desperate after the opposition candidate he led the campaign for lost. His dream of a lucrative government position also vanished.'

'But ... but how did he know where I was and who I was? I haven't seen him for over two decades!'

Chief Panalo straightened himself again. 'Well, he has

his resources, obviously. Apparently, he saw you on the TV when you accompanied your cousin for the interview about missing Nina. He then had you followed.'

Hearing this information brought chills to Maya's bones. 'Oh, my word, th … the bastard! I want him to rot in jail forever!' Maya at last let out her anger as Keith held her trembling hands.

Chapter Thirty

The next morning, Maya and Keith went to the police headquarters to sign more documents. The case against the abductors was to be filed by the state on behalf of the victims, including Maya, but she needed to sign legal paperwork so she could avoid being present at the court trials.

Maya and Keith planned to leave for the province the following day and they were on their way back to their hotel when Maya's phone rang. It was Elena, Tito Eddy's wife.

'Hello, Maya dear, we're at the Manuela Hospital. Your Tito is fading rapidly and the doctors say he might not last the day.' Tita Elena was sobbing between words.

'Oh, I'm so sorry to hear that, Tita,' Maya said. 'We'll be there as soon as we can. Keep your faith.' Although Maya had tried to convince Tita Elena and herself that everything was going to be OK, she was disturbed and worried. She hadn't expected her old mentor to deteriorate this quickly. She told Keith about the call and he instructed the taxi driver to take them straight to the hospital.

Tito Eddy was in the Intensive Care Unit when Maya and Keith arrived. A distraught Tita Elena greeted them. All their family and close friends were in the lobby. Although frail, Tita Elena accompanied the couple to her husband's room once the previous visitor had come out.

Surrounded by medical equipment, Tito Eddy looked such a tiny figure. A little plastic tube ran from his nose and mouth and his eyes were closed. Tita Elena whispered into his ear that Maya and Keith were with them. His eyelids moved, indicating that he had heard her. Maya held his hands and couldn't contain her tears.

'Thank you, Tito, for everything. I wouldn't be the person I am today if not for you. I have always loved you as my father.'

Maya couldn't stop her tears and Keith gave her a tissue. He didn't know Tito Eddy as well as Maya, but he had always liked and respected him as an older relative. He'd also been the main sponsor for their wedding.

After a few minutes, Tito Eddy let out a big breath before his head slumped to the left. A prolonged beeping noise came from the machine he was attached to and a number of medical staff rushed into the room. Tita Elena wailed as she hugged her dearest husband. Maya kissed his forehead and Keith held his hand while murmuring 'goodbye'. Then the three of them were ushered out of the room.

Tito Eddy's family and friends guessed what had happened and nothing could be heard but quiet cries of deep sorrow for the loss of a much-loved husband, father, brother, relative, friend and mentor. Tito Eddy was a true media professional and an inspiration to many.

For Maya, the four-hour journey to the province seemed to take forever. She wanted to be out of the city as soon as possible. The death of her father figure and long-time friend was the latest blow among many. Tito Eddy's funeral wouldn't be for a few days, so they decided to visit the province first, as planned.

'When it rains it pours, eh?' Maya stated as she and Keith sat in the back passenger seats of their hired vehicle.

'Yes, but remember the old adage that there's always a light at the end of the tunnel,' Keith interjected.

'Always!' Maya replied and gave a half-hearted laugh.

Instead of taking public transport, they'd decided to hire a vehicle so they could stop for a rest whenever they needed to. The driver and his assistant, who was seated next to him, were very pleasant and tried to entertain their passengers with the occasional joke to break the monotony of the journey. They stopped at a service station restaurant for lunch and made a few more stops to appreciate the fresh atmosphere of their hilly, provincial surroundings.

Chapter Thirty One

It was nearly 4pm by the time Maya and Keith reached the town of Liwag. Auntie Lina's house was a mile away from Maya's ancestral home, so they went there first. As Maya got out of the car, Nina ran out to greet her and Maya picked her up and took her inside. Auntie Lina's house was very busy, with many people milling about working on things. When Maya enquired what was going on, Auntie Lina explained that they were preparing for a special event the following evening, to be held within their compound. She and Uncle Larry had decided to throw a thanksgiving and homecoming party for Cora and her kids, to celebrate them returning to live in the province. They'd scheduled it while Maya and Keith were in town, and Maya couldn't wait. She missed attending parties the provincial way and was excited about the event to come.

They stayed at Auntie Lina's house for half an hour before heading towards Maya's ancestral home. As they approached it, Maya felt an all too familiar mixture of sadness and joy. This was a very precious place to her, where she felt closest to her parents. Out of all the properties she'd inherited, she considered this the best one and would never get rid of it. She planned to eventually pass it on to her goddaughter, Nina.

The house was huge; a typical, Spanish-influenced Filipino home that had stood the test of time for decades. Four wide white columns at the entrance formed the big porch, where her father used to sit and relax every evening. Above it was an equally large balcony, which led off from the first floor family room. The building frames and walls were made from concrete, which were complemented by the wooden windows. They fully opened outwards, bringing fresh air into the house.

The ground floor consisted of a huge *sala* or living room, a big kitchen and a dining room. It also contained a separate, two-bedroom, fully fitted living space where the caretakers resided. The upstairs comprised five large bedrooms, one of which was Maya's. Her room overlooked a large and well-maintained back garden that housed a variety of fruit trees and a small pond. It still contained some of her early years and school memoirs, which her mother had collected. In the family room upstairs was a table filled with old framed photographs. There was a large photo of Maya's parents taken on their wedding day and hanging on the wall was a beautiful one of Maya when she was a toddler.

Manang Bev and her husband *Manong* Nardo greeted Maya and Keith as they arrived. They'd been the caretakers of the house since Maya's parents died and she'd gone to live with her auntie and uncle. The couple did an outstanding job of keeping the house shipshape, which is just the way Maya would have done it. They took care of it as their own. Maya's occasional visits were always a delight to them and they prepared all the meals for her and her guests. Keith had been there several times before and he loved the place. He'd never met Maya's parents, but he felt close to them there, too.

After getting settled in the house and before they had dinner, Maya and Keith's driver and his assistant, who were staying in one of the guestrooms, took them to the cemetery so Maya could lay flowers at her parents' graves. She loved spending time sitting in silence at their resting place and talking to them in her head. Keith usually left her alone in her contemplation.

This time, Maya noticed that some fresh flowers had been put on the grave. She was puzzled, as she was usually the only one who left flowers there.

Back at the house, Maya and Keith enjoyed a delectable dinner with the caretakers, the driver and his assistant. Even though they hardly knew each other it was nice to eat in a group. *Manong* Nardo turned out to be a bit of a joker, as was the driver's assistant. Together they filled the dining room with laughter.

The following day was the party for Cora and her kids. A large DIY marquee had been erected outside the house and a big canvas roof held up by poles covered most of the outside area. Plastic chairs and wooden benches had been set out for visitors to sit on. There was also a designated stage area.

A mass was heard at 3pm before the full party programme began. At 7pm, dinner was served. Many people attended, including friends, neighbours, relatives and acquaintances. It was a typical party in the province in that it was open to virtually everyone in town. The dancing, singing and drinking went on until 10pm, when everyone started to leave. One of the last people to go was an elderly man. Maya had seen him earlier and thought he looked too drunk to be left to his own devices. She was pleased when someone turned up to take him home.

Everyone had a great time, especially Nina and Dino, who enjoyed being fussed over. There were many other kids present and they got together to make their own entertainment. Most of them went home after dinner, but some stayed and joined in with the dancing, including Nina and Dino.

The following day, Maya and Keith woke up late, both suffering from a bit of a hangover. They decided to go to the nearby beach and invited Cora and her kids. It was a beautiful day for lazing about and there were vendors nearby to buy food and drinks from. They returned to their shelter and enjoyed a picnic, staying at the beach for most of the afternoon to swim and sunbathe. The sea breeze meant it never became too hot.

On their way back home, Maya and her group stopped

by the cemetery gates and Keith accompanied Maya as she walked to her parents' final resting place. She noticed this time that there was a fresh white rose on the grave. She wished she knew who was leaving the flowers so she could show her appreciation. She'd mentioned it to the caretakers and to Auntie Lina and Uncle Larry, but they didn't have a clue who was behind the gesture; it certainly wasn't them or anyone they knew. Maya was all the more intrigued.

As Maya and Keith walked back to their waiting car, they noticed a man walking ahead of them. He kept looking back. As they got closer to him, they noticed he was the drunken elderly man who'd been at the party. He looked at Maya intently.

'Are you OK, *tatang*?' Maya asked.

The man hesitated, but kept staring at Maya. She decided he must be in his 70s. He looked very frail and had an extremely wrinkly face. He was also walking very slowly.

'*Nakong*, I'm so sorry,' the elderly man finally said.

'For what, *tatang*? Are you a relative?'

The elderly man shook his head. 'I need to talk to you and ask for your forgiveness,' he said meekly, while still looking into Maya's eyes.

'What are you talking about?' The encounter was beginning to make her feel uncomfortable.

'I killed your parents,' the elderly man said bluntly before suddenly dropping to his knees in front of Maya. 'Please forgive me, *nakong*. I cannot bear this anymore. I've waited a long time for this opportunity to see you and I cannot let it pass. I am so sorry for what I have done.'

Maya was totally astounded. She didn't know what to say. Feelings of hurt and pity were battling within her.

Keith helped the elderly man get to his feet. 'I think we better go to the police station, sir,' he said.

The elderly man was called Pablo and he was duly questioned at the police station. Maya and Keith were allowed to listen in. It transpired that he was one of the three hitmen hired by an ardent opponent of Maya's father during the mayoral elections. He didn't go on to win because he was rumoured to have been behind the deaths of Mayor Wara and his wife Elizabeth, even though the coroner concluded they had lost their lives in an accident.

The elderly Pablo recounted how he and his two accomplices followed Mayor Wara's movements for at least a few days. He and his wife were driving home from an evening meeting with the local community when Pablo and the two other men drove towards him from the opposite direction. They were on a bend and Pablo put his headlights onto full beam, which blinded Maya's father and caused him to plunge his car into a ravine. The hitmen checked that Mr Wara and his wife had no chance of survival before speeding off.

The elderly man was clearly remorseful as he spoke and kept looking at Maya, who was staring at the floor whilst Keith listened intently. It was likely that everyone else involved in the crime had passed away. Maya's father's opponent, who paid Pablo and his accomplices to commit the crime, was dead and, as far as Pablo knew, he was the only one of the hitmen still alive. He had lost contact with them years earlier when he'd decided to clean up his act and start a family. He was now determined to tell the truth and had prayed for this opportunity.

After the police interview, Pablo was taken into police custody and Maya and Keith headed home. That night, Maya couldn't sleep. Keith gave her the space to think and decide for herself if she was going to pursue a case against one of her parents' killers. He told her that he would support her whatever decision she made.

Maya thought how she should be elated that finally her parents were going to get justice, only she didn't feel vengeful towards the old man; instead she felt pity for him and even a twinge of admiration for how he'd admitted to the crime. Her parents would have almost been the same age as the elderly Pablo, and Maya wondered what they would tell her to do if she were able to speak to them. She decided to wait until the following day and see how she felt then.

The next morning, Maya and Keith went to the police station and spoke to the officer in charge. After a while, Pablo was brought out from the cell and into the reception area. He walked over to Maya and was about to drop to his knees again when Maya stopped him.

'*Tatang*, go home and enjoy your family,' she said firmly.

'Thank you ever so much, *nakong*. I can rest forever now

with peace in my heart.' Pablo had a tear in his eye as he spoke.

On their final day in the province, Maya and Keith bade goodbye to their family and friends. Before their journey back to Manila, Maya went to lay a bunch of fresh and beautiful white roses on her parents' grave. As she did so, she felt strangely happy.

'Rest in peace forever now, Pa and Ma,' she murmured as she kissed the flowers and gently placed them on the grave beside the single rose that Pablo had left there.

Chapter Thirty Two

Back in Manila, Maya and Keith went to Tito Eddy's funeral. Gina, Edward and almost all of Maya's former colleagues were there. St Mary's Cathedral, where the service was held, was so full to the brim that people had to stand up at the back.

In addition, many of Tito Eddy's fans across the archipelago crowded the grounds and streets surrounding the cathedral. The police hadn't anticipated the sheer number of fans and extra officers were drafted in to assist pedestrians and deal with the traffic.

News of Tito Eddy's funeral made headlines in most leading newspapers and on radio and television stations. It was also all over social media. One of the moving articles read:

The remarkable, outstanding and outspoken darling of the news and radio industries, Dr Eduardo Franco, famously known as Tito Eddy by his friends, colleagues and fans, was laid to rest today.

Farewell our beloved Tito Eddy. Your legacy of truthful, trustworthy and ethical news and information distribution through the media will always remain. You are the epitome of a true model for all aspiring future media personalities. Thank you.

Chief Superintendent Panalo was also at the funeral service. At the private gathering afterwards, for family, relatives and close friends, he took the chance to inform Keith and Maya that Brian Philips, who was being held at the Pootan Detention Centre, would be able to return to the UK in a few weeks. He would not pay any charges, as he had already spent more than enough time in detention – time that could never be bought back. The cases against him were dropped.

Chief Panalo also said that the IB's legal team added in their resolution to the President that foreigners would have the right to keep their properties, especially if they were not married to their partners. It was most likely that Brian would eventually get most, if not all, of his properties and belongings back from his ex-girlfriend.

Chapter Thirty Three

Maya and Keith decided to visit Puerto Galla for a couple of nights before heading back to Scotland. This time, they travelled by air and within half an hour they had reached the island where they first met. They took a taxi to the Beachfront Hotel and arrived there in just 15 minutes.

Maya noticed that although tricycles were still taking passengers about on the island, yellow taxis were now more prominent. The island had completely changed since she and Keith were last there for their wedding. Many hotels and large buildings had gone up and the roads were a lot wider and had street lights. The Hilltop Cottages complex was no longer there and in its place stood the massive Hilltop Hotel. Their driver told them it was one of the most luxurious contemporary hotels on the island. Maya felt a bit disappointed that she wasn't able to visit the first place she'd lived on her favourite island.

Mr and Mrs Davies were delighted to welcome the couple. Their hotel was even more beautiful than Maya remembered. She'd stayed at many luxurious hotels in her time, but nothing compared to the Beachfront.

Once they were settled into their penthouse room, Mr and Mrs Davies invited them for dinner in their residence. After their scrumptious meal, Keith and Mr Davies caught up while Maya and Mrs Davies chatted amongst themselves.

Mrs Davies explained how they had maintained the status of their luxurious hotel all these years but were planning to retire in ten years' time. Their two children weren't interested in taking over the family business. Their daughter was training to be a medical doctor in Makati and their son was an engineer working and living in Bago City with his young family. Mr and Mrs Davies planned to stay on the island after retirement, sell their hotel and downsize. They also wanted to travel the world.

The next morning, when Maya and Keith went down to the restaurant for their breakfast, they saw a young, good-looking police officer at reception. They were heading to the grand staircase when the man approached them.

'Good morning, Mr Smith and *Ate* Maya,' he said, with a somewhat familiar tone.

Maya quickly realised who the man was – it was Junior! 'Oh my goodness, it's you!' she exclaimed, giving him a hug.

Keith smiled. 'I knew you would do it, young man,' he

said as he shook Junior's hand and also embraced him.

'We're on our way for breakfast,' Maya said, checking out Junior's smart uniform from head to toe. 'Do you want to join us and we'll catch up? That is, if you're available, of course.'

Maya noticed that his badge read, 'Renato Banawa Jr, Officer In Charge, The Philippine Police Force.'

'I'm on duty in an hour's time,' Junior explained. 'I heard yesterday that you had arrived on the island and I thought I'd come and see you first thing today. Of course I'll join you, but I'll only have a coffee as I ate at home.'

As they sat together, Junior updated Maya and Keith on their old island friends. Renato had sadly passed away three years earlier and Junior's mother, Josefa, now lived with his youngest sister, Josie, who ran a successful restaurant on the island. His sister Leona was a local schoolteacher while his third, Maria, was a nurse working in the USA.

After training to be a police officer, Junior was assigned to various areas of Luzon. He met his wife Celia during one of his assignments in the Cordilleras. When they started a family, he asked to be permanently assigned to his hometown, which he'd always wanted to serve. He, his wife and their two girls had been on the island for five years now. The former Officer in Charge had been relocated the previous year and Junior was promoted to his new position, which meant he was currently in charge of 10 other officers.

'Oh, I'm so proud of you, Junior! I'm sure Renato would be too,' Maya said. 'And he should be proud of himself too for bringing you all up and making sure you were properly educated. That must have taken hard work and perseverance.'

As Keith nodded his approval, Maya felt sad that she would never be able to compliment Renato in person.

Junior happily informed Maya and Keith that Aida, the former shopkeeper who'd once helped investigate the paedophile ring, now owned one of the biggest grocery shops on the island. Berto, the porter, had moved back to his native Cawayan province to start a restaurant business with his family.

'So I guess you must be enjoying your job, then,' Keith said with a grin. 'Years ago you told us you wanted to be a policeman and now look at you – you've fulfilled your dream!'

'Oh, yes, totally, Mr Smith! I love my job, but being the new OIC of the police force on the island has been both challenging and rewarding. I was so happy when I got the promotion. This is my chance to realise another dream – to lead my island to become a much better and peaceful place to live and visit.'

Junior went on to explain that the island hadn't been spared any of the major problems that the country had as a whole. In fact, after the exposure of the paedophile ring, a rehabilitation centre was built for all those who'd been affected. It was available to all ages and was run by a charity foundation. Over the years, many people had sought help and turned their lives around. The centre was located a few miles from the rocky beaches where Maya and Keith had enjoyed a picnic with Renato and Junior.

'Our picnic area!' said Maya. 'What a memorable day that was, eh? I certainly think that area is suitable for rehabilitation purposes – it was so very peaceful and relaxing.'

Keith and Junior both nodded with broad smiles on their faces. They also had flashbacks of their momentous picnic at a perfect spot.

Junior abruptly cut short their reminiscing and carried on with his narration. 'As the issue of paedophilia waned,' he explained, 'the problem of illegal drugs started. It began with visitors from the cities or the mainland, who came to the island for short holidays and brought *shabu* with them.' He paused and sipped his coffee. 'Over the years, the island was a perfect hideaway for drug users and dealers. In fact, a couple of illegal drug factories were raided here after the President declared his FAID campaign. Consequently, the rehabilitation centre expanded and the charity foundation partnered with the local government. It's currently used to rehabilitate both local drug addicts and some brought here from nearby mainland areas.'

Junior sighed as he related the current social issues on the island, which were the same as most of the nation.

'Looks like you're on the right track with it, though,' Keith observed.

'Thanks, Mr Smith,' Junior replied. 'I really hope our President's FAID campaign serves its purposes. It looks promising at the moment, but another matter that has bugged the island for years is the environmental issue.' He paused and took another sip of his coffee. 'With so many big hotels and businesses popping up each year, the environment has suffered quite drastically. Much of the forest has been cleared for building work and the sea has been polluted due to the lack of a proper sewerage system. But then again, I'm hopeful and positive that the new policies implemented by the Environmental Department, which my police department has to strictly monitor, will be successful.'

Junior checked his watch. 'Sorry, *Ate* Maya and Mr Smith, I need to go now.'

As the young officer stood up, Keith got up from his chair and took off his Bulgari diver's watch. He gave it to Junior. 'Please take it, it's my small gift to you. You've done very well in your life and may you carry on your good deeds forever.'

Junior was hesitant at first, but Keith persuaded him to accept the expensive present. 'Thank you so much, Mr Smith. You are such a kind person.'

Junior chuckled as he looked at the simple yet elegant watch and gingerly put it on his right wrist.

Maya stood up and hugged Junior. 'We're going back to Manila at midday tomorrow so we may not see you. Take care always, Junior, and look after your family too. Hopefully we'll return in the near future.'

Maya genuinely cared for this young man, who was like the brother she'd never had. 'Add me to your Facebook if you have one, and we'll keep in touch, OK?'

'Yes, *Ate*, I have one and I will,' Junior smiled.

'Bye for now,' Keith said and the two men shook hands.

Chapter Thirty Four

Maya and Keith spent the rest of the day retracing some of their old steps on the island. They had a lovely lunch at the Hilltop Hotel's balcony restaurant, which overlooked the beach and sea. Both were reminded of the perfect view that Maya had enjoyed in her old rented cottage over two decades ago.

Across from the Hilltop Hotel was a one-storey building with a sparkly sign that read, *Aida's Grocery Shop.* After lunch, the couple went to visit it. Their old friend was overwhelmed to see them. She was as chatty as ever and updated the couple from where they had left off.

The island had had its ups and downs, but it had been good for the local people and the economy in general. Nowadays, almost all the locals had a job. As Junior had explained, many of the abuse victims had received help at the rehabilitation centre and turned their lives around.

'Remember Edith, who was nine when you knew her?' Aida asked Maya.

'Oh yes, of course I do! She was the girl I met at the swimming pool. How is she now?'

Aida smiled. 'Well, would you believe she's now in her early 30s and one of the people in charge of the centre. Unfortunately, though, over the years her mother Betty went crazy and eventually killed herself. Apparently, she couldn't handle the fact that she allowed her children to be abused by her paedophile boyfriend.'

'Oh my, I'm sorry for the mother, that's very sad,' Maya remarked.

'Yes, it's very sad indeed,' said Aida. 'Edith and her sisters were helped by the people at the centre and now they have their own jobs and families.' Sensing that she might sound like a typical gossip, Aida explained further. 'Everyone on the island knows Edith and her sisters' stories, and I'm always happy to share them too, because they are a good example of how you can make a success of yourself despite life's trials and tribulations.'

'Wow, I'm delighted to hear that,' Maya beamed. Keith was smiling too as he listened intently to Aida's animated conversation.

'By the way, if there was a paedophile lurking on this island nowadays, they would be found sooner rather than later because every single resident here has been educated about the issue and would know how to spot one. Furthermore, our *Anak*, the new police OIC – you know him

– would find these assholes all right. We all call Junior *Anak* because he is the very first OIC from our island. We're so proud of him!'

Maya was so happy to be able to chat with Aida after all these years. She was the island's walking newspaper, and rightly so. The shop was getting busy and one of Aida's staff members kept coming out to see if she was available, so Maya decided they should leave. 'I see you're very busy,' she said. 'But I just want to add how happy I am to see the success you have made of yourself.'

'Thank you, I really enjoy what I do,' Aida replied.

'And being happy is a success in itself,' Keith added.

Aida smiled and became pensive for a moment. 'You know what, the island is indebted to both of you for what you did for us. You helped drive those paedophiles away and our island is such a better place in that sense.'

'We were just doing what we thought was the right thing,' Maya said. 'But we're glad to see that so many improvements have been made since our time here.'

Aida seemed to have much more information to share. 'Of course, there are still some other social issues, like *shabu*, which unfortunately affected us as much as the mainland. But I'm hopeful that our dear President's campaign will eventually eradicate it.'

After a few more minutes of chatting, Maya and Keith bade their goodbyes once again. As usual, Aida was tearful and said she hoped to see them both again soon. She even suggested they should move to the island, which Keith said they'd think about.

The couple picked up a tricycle and asked to be dropped off at the road nearest to the Cava Cave. From there, it was about a five-hundred-metre climb to their destination. The hill that led to the cave was barer than before and the path leading to it was a lot wider and smoother. Barbed wire fencing surrounded the area around a hundred metres from the cave and there was a clear path to follow towards its entrance. The bats were under protection and this was clear when Maya and Keith walked in and were met by the noise of hundreds of them flying about.

Keith enjoyed taking photos of Maya and for the first time ever he took a selfie of them together in the place where they met. They sat for a few minutes where years ago they had once spoken as strangers, and they joked about their adventures – or Keith's misadventure – on that day. Afterwards, they walked back down the path and followed the sign to the waterfall. The place was as majestic as ever, even though some barriers had been put up to prevent accidents. A viewing platform had been erected at the top of the rock, which they'd sat together on once before. They remained there mesmerised by the place before taking some more photographs.

It was late in the afternoon by the time Maya and Keith headed down the hill to town. Despite building work, they had a good feeling about the changes occurring on the island. They walked towards the beach and had a swim in the sea before continuing on towards the Beachfront Hotel in their sopping clothes. They changed in their room before going for dinner at the restaurant. To everyone who saw them, it was obvious that they were one happy and contented couple.

Later, Keith stood behind Maya at the large, familiar window of their penthouse room. They watched the sunset together, arms entwined.

'Life is full of surprises, and every sunset brings a new dawn,' Maya murmured as Keith lovingly carried her to the bed.

> *Two people, two souls*
> *Entwined by their hearts*
> *For the love they found*
> *On an island they adored.*
>
> *Through sadness and thrill*
> *Endured the test of times*
> *Like rocks stood still*
> *Amidst raging waters.*
>
> *Love has given them the chance*
> *To live life and carry on.*
>
> *As their bed creaked*
> *Their souls rejoiced*
> *And waited for another dawn.*

EPILOGUE

JANUARY 2018 – Alban, Highlands of Scotland

It had been a very busy and happy Christmas for the Smith household. Keith's daughter Penny, who was now in her mid-20s, and her husband, Peter, came over from South Africa and stayed with them for two weeks. Despite the snowy weather, the four of them managed to visit some interesting places and took a skiing trip to Aviemore. The young couple had a brilliant time and planned to tour the whole country one summer in the near future.

After Penny and Peter left, Keith and Maya went for a nice wintry evening walk with their two Shih-Tzu dogs, Jani and Jano. When they got back home, Maya made herself a hot chocolate, switched on her laptop and checked her emails.

The first email came from her cousin Cora.

My dearest, *Manang* Maya,

Greetings to you and Keith and wishing you both a Happy New Year! I hope you're both well, as we all are. The kids have settled in very well at their new schools and my dental clinic, which is the only one in town, is doing very well so far. Mom and Dad are doing fine, although Dad is very forgetful nowadays. They love having the kids here, who keep our two oldies very busy indeed.

As you know, I met up with my childhood sweetheart, Nolan Rivera, a week after we moved to the province. I didn't know that he'd never married! We get on very well and the spark in my life has returned. Over the last few months, he's been a regular visitor to our house and the kids adore him. And there's more. He proposed on New Year's Eve and we're getting married in June! Please make your diary available, *Manang*, OK?

Speak to you soon.

Love and miss you lots,

Cora

Maya chuckled and had tears in her eyes. She was so pleased that her dear cousin, her little sister, had finally found happiness again. She finished drinking her hot chocolate and carried on reading her other emails. Her eyes brightened when she saw Gina's name.

Hey, Maya dear!

Happy 2018 to you and Keith! Hope you're both well. ☺

Just a little update from here …

The country is starting to reap the rewards of the current administration's efforts:

- Infrastructure is on the up.

- New railways and roads are on the map.

- New international airports are soon to open.

- Tuition fees for students at state schools are now free.

- Crime rates are continuing to drop.

- The use and spread of illegal drugs is still going on, but it's not as rampant as it was two years ago, thanks to the President's ongoing war against it.

- Tourism is booming; three big cruise ships arrived in Manila recently. I couldn't have imagined that five years ago.

- There are so many more good things happening here.

I want to tell you not to believe everything you read and hear via the international media regarding the negative stuff that is constantly reported about our country and our dear President; it's our country, we live here – they live somewhere else. Unless they have lived here, they can know nothing about us. Their sources are usually the biased local media here. What is it called? Black Propaganda?

Nearly two years after the elections, a few groups of politicians and non-government organisations are continuing their insane campaign to malign our President in order to grab the power given to him by a DEMOCRATIC country. Why do you think they are making such an incessant effort? Hah! My gut feeling is that these power-grabbers want to resume their illicit and self-serving activities, and to continue to succumb to the demands of the oligarchs – the only ones who have flourished over the last few decades. They want to continue depriving the common people and future generations of a better chance in life. How dare they? Our people voted in our President because they believed in him, and he has so far delivered on many of his promises to the people and our country.

By the way, with regards to the suggestion you made in your previous email, we're in the final stages of our research regarding immigration anomalies. We've compiled the cases of some of the foreign detainees at the Pootan Detention Centre and will be featuring them in my talk shows next month. I hope the pressure we'll put on the relevant government agencies will have a positive result. I will keep you updated.

And yes, the country is preparing for another election next year for the senatorial seats. Some people suggested I should run, which I found hilarious. No thank you! I am happy with my current job and only hope people will have a good idea of who to vote for.

In less than two years, the current administration has made many changes for the better in our country, but a lot more needs to be done. People's openness to the concept that 'change is coming' seems to be favourable in general. But people must realise that first and foremost change comes from within, right? I'm sure you agree with that, my friend. ☺

There is widespread hope, so onwards and upwards for the future BETTERMENT of our beloved nation.

And another thing, at the end of last year, the Chinese hostage that you were locked up with was finally repatriated to his homeland. The other man – the one who had surrendered for drug dealing offences – applied to be rehabilitated. Apparently, he seemed very sincere about changing his lifestyle for the sake of his family. Your abductors were jailed for life and Arthur got life too – without parole.

And, before I forget, Eric and I are celebrating our 15th wedding anniversary in July and we've decided to tour Europe, so I hope to see you in the UK in the summer.

Catch up soon and take care.

Love,

Gina

Maya smiled and started to type …

GLOSSARY

Ate – Used to address an older sister. Also a younger person's sign of respect to address an older female, who is usually younger by a few years only.

Barangay – The native Filipino term for a village.

Filipina – Used when referring to a female from the Philippines.

Filipino – Used in various ways: (noun) A native or an inhabitant of the Philippines, used as a collective term to describe the people in the Philippines; (noun) term for the national language of the Philippines; (adjective) describes the people, food, culture etc; also used to refer to a male person from the Philippines.

Lola – The term for grandmother. Also used for other elderly relatives and close friends.

Lolo – The term for grandfather. Also used for other elderly relatives and close friends.

Manang – A vernacular version of Ate, it's mostly used in the northern part of the Philippines.

Manong – The male version of Manang.

Nakong – The local term for a child in some northern parts of the Philippines. Also used by someone who feels a special affection for the addressee.

Pandesal – The most popular type of bread roll in the Philippines, it's baked using flour, eggs, yeast, sugar and salt.

Sala – The Filipino term for a living room.

Sapinit – Wild raspberry.

Shabu – The local term for the illegal drug crystal methamphetamine, a very destructive stimulant that affects the central nervous system.

Tatang – This is the local term for a father in some northern parts of the Philippines. Also used by someone who feels a special affection for the addressee, or to show respect to an elderly man.

Tita – The term for an aunt or stepmother. Also used as a sign of respect to address an older female, who usually has an affiliation with the addressor.

Tito – The term for an uncle or stepfather. Also used as a sign of respect to address an older male, who usually has an affiliation with the addressor.

Tricycle – A three-wheeled vehicle made up of a motorcycle and a covered carriage on wheels attached to its side. It's a common and cheap form of public transport for short distances in most parts of the Philippines.

About The Author

Emikat Jun was born in Lamut, Ifugao, and grew up in Balbalan, Kalinga, in the highland provinces of the Philippines. Her father introduced her to literature when she was at primary school by training her in Declamation (Monologue) to compete against other schools during district competitions. From a very young age, she was fond of listening to folktales and other stories narrated by older relatives and friends.

Emikat gained an accounting degree in the Philippines before moving to the UK in 1995, where she worked in finance. While working and raising a child as a single parent, after her first marriage failed, she found time to pursue her childhood passion and studied for a degree in English Language and Literature. She went on to gain her Masters in MLitt Highlands and Islands Literature.

Today, *Emikat* lives in Coatbridge, Scotland, UK. Since her move to Britain, she has travelled to the Philippines several times to visit relatives and friends.

Behind The Mask is her debut novel.